Vi McConne...
↟ER Vera   pe...

‖‖‖‖‖‖‖‖‖‖‖
☑ S0-CDO-834

*A Candlelight
Ecstasy Romance*®

"YOU'VE DECIDED THAT I'M UP TO NO GOOD, HAVEN'T YOU?" MAX SAID, AS HE SMILED DOWN AT HER.

"I've . . . given the matter an occasional thought," she admitted.

"Only a thought?" he teased.

"I can't decide if you're a bank robber, an escaped convict hiding from the authorities, or some wild eccentric involved in a nefarious plot to overthrow the government. I know nothing about you at all!"

Yet despite her protests and suspicions Shena was painfully attracted to him. But how could she be falling in love with a man who was such a mystery?

CANDLELIGHT ECSTASY ROMANCES®

RELENTLESS PURSUIT

Eleanor Woods

A CANDLELIGHT ECSTASY ROMANCE®

Published by
Dell Publishing Co., Inc.
1 Dag Hammarskjold Plaza
New York, New York 10017

Copyright © 1985 by Eleanor Woods

All rights reserved. No part of this book may be reproduced
or transmitted in any form or by any means, electronic or
mechanical, including photocopying, recording, or by any
information storage and retrieval system, without the written
permission of the Publisher, except where permitted by law.

Dell ® TM 681510, Dell Publishing Co., Inc.

Candlelight Ecstasy Romance®, 1,203,540, is a registered
trademark of Dell Publishing Co., Inc., New York, New York.

ISBN: 0-440-17434-1

Printed in the United States of America

First printing—August 1985

To Our Readers:

We have been delighted with your enthusiastic response to Candlelight Ecstasy Romances®, and we thank you for the interest you have shown in this exciting series.

In the upcoming months we will continue to present the distinctive, sensuous love stories you have come to expect only from Ecstasy. We look forward to bringing you many more books from your favorite authors and also the very finest work from new authors of contemporary romantic fiction.

As always, we are striving to present the unique, absorbing love stories that you enjoy most—books that are more than ordinary romance. Your suggestions and comments are always welcome. Please write to us at the address below.

Sincerely,

The Editors
Candlelight Romances
1 Dag Hammarskjold Plaza
New York, New York 10017

CHAPTER ONE

Despite Shena McLean's certainty that every tooth in her head was quickly and systematically being loosened from its place due to her mode of transportation, the infectious grin on her lightly freckled face never wavered. There was a sparkling freshness about her mop of curly auburn hair and her slight jean-clad figure that seemed strangely at odds with the mysterious slant of her teasing blue eyes.

Today those eyes were lit with excitement. Even the dilapidated old pickup truck she was driving and the steady drizzle of rain that was falling failed to cast a blemish on her day. The city of Jacksonville was behind her, forgotten till Monday morning. She had two days to try and finish the cabin . . . and perhaps fish in the late afternoon in Willow Creek. The small stream was fed by one of the numerous underwater springs Florida was famous for and emptied into the St. John River. Her cabin and one other sat in a curve of the creek, almost two miles from any of the cabins whose owners came yearly to the area.

She gave a quick glance in the rearview mirror to

make sure the piece of heavy plastic covering the lumber she was hauling was still in place. Considering the price she'd paid for those boards, she sighed, they should have been wrapped in gold paper and tied with a red velvet bow. If she and Win really pushed it, they could get the closet in the bedroom roughed in. If he shows up. Shena frowned as she pictured her blond-headed, short, stocky best friend. Lawrence Winfield Logan. His father was a banker, his mother one of the local leaders of society. Win? She smiled fondly. If someone hadn't made a place for him, he would have become a bum. From time to time he seemed to need almost as much shoring up as the cabin they'd worked so hard on.

It was strange, she mused as she slowed down and made the turn off the main highway onto a dirt road, the gears of the old truck protesting noisily. All she seemed to be doing these days was either reworking, rebuilding or patching up something. She was beginning to think the whole darn world was in need of repair!

As if to reenforce her thoughts, the truck chose that particular moment to let forth a metal-grinding noise that made Shena jerk forward, a look of determination on her face.

Just a little farther, she thought coaxingly, her hands gripping the steering wheel. Just a little farther.

Her foot pressed harder on the accelerator in hopes of getting as close to the cabin as possible in case her pockmarked, fender-bent vehicle decided to give up the ghost. The added pressure brought a sudden burst of speed to the truck, and a grateful Shena momentarily relaxed.

The road to the cabin came into view. Without more than the barest touch of her foot on the brake, she took the turn on two wheels. So far, so good, she congratulated herself as she fought to bring the pickup back to the center of the road, narrowly avoiding a head-on collision with a sturdy pine tree.

Like a race-car driver at Indy, Shena immediately jammed the accelerator to the floor, determined to make the last mile of her journey on four wheels rather than on two feet. She crossed her fingers as the last hurdle of her journey came into view. It was a hill, not a really big one, but big enough to halt the forward progress of her temperamental truck if she wasn't careful.

A thrill of victory raced through her veins as she neared the top of the incline. But she was so busy glancing through the window behind her to check on the lumber, and praising her own expert driving, she failed to see the vehicle approaching ahead of her.

One moment the narrow road was clear, the next, a dark blue car lay directly in her path.

The ensuing moments would always remain somewhat cloudy in her mind. The only clear and concise thing she did remember was trying desperately to turn the steering wheel to the right. Unfortunately, the steering wheel had become inoperable, rendering it useless except as an excellent handle upon which to cling as she began an entirely new and unchartered route toward the cabin.

She caught a brief glimpse of the driver of the car. His expression was one of incredulity as the right front bumper of the pickup truck became a hungry beast and neatly wrenched off the fender from his shiny new car with an ear-splitting screech.

With safety her number one priority, Shena loosened her grip on the steering wheel and flung her body sideways along the seat, desperately trying to brace herself against the impact to come.

At first she was certain she was flying! Then there was a bone-wrenching jolt and her journey was abruptly halted. Shena remained motionless, her body frozen. The only sound she heard was the falling rain hitting the cab.

Suddenly the door on the driver's side was flung open and she was conscious of water dripping on her ankles. It was very uncomfortable, she thought irritably, having a river of rain run into one's shoes. Before she could move her feet, however, she felt the firm clasp of hands running over her legs, her thighs and working their way upward.

"Please," she managed to cry out before every inch of her was gone over, "I think I'm okay!"

"Well now, I sure as hell don't see how that's possible," a deep, thoroughly annoyed male voice replied, booming in the stillness brought about by the sudden halting of the rain. He did, however, remove his hands.

Shena wiggled and squirmed until her arms were free of the weight of her body, then cautiously pushed herself into a sitting position. She turned to find herself staring into the most remarkable face she'd ever seen.

The man's hair was light brown and, at the moment, lying thick and straight and wet against his scalp. His forehead was wide, his brows heavy and drawn together in a dark, thunderous line.

There was open hostility in the hazel eyes glaring at her. Shena took a deep, trembling breath as her own eyes continued their slow scrutiny of a nose that could only be called large, a mouth she was certain could smile but probably didn't very often and a chin and jaw so strong, so unyielding as to defy description.

Lord! she sighed shakily. I do believe I've been rescued by a damned Viking! And an unfriendly one at that. Though thinking over the last few minutes, she really could see why he might be a teeny bit upset with her.

"I really am sorry about your car," she offered in a level voice.

"The car can be repaired," he replied shortly. "It was my personal safety I was concerned with." He extended a large, steady hand to her. "Unless you intend to set up house in this damn wreck, I'd suggest you get out and make sure you really are all right."

13

Shena was tempted to ignore the offer, but after catching a glimpse of his car, she decided she shouldn't antagonize the man. The late-model Lincoln was minus one front fender, and the side panel had a deep, ugly gouge in it.

She turned back to the angry person glaring at her. He looked mean enough and mad enough to tangle with a rattlesnake—and win!

The moment her feet touched the rain-soaked ground, Shena became aware of the disparity in their heights. The "gentleman" assisting her was huge as an oak tree. The light blue work shirt he was wearing clung wet and close to his body like a second skin, the muscles in his powerful shoulders stretching the material taut with each movement of his long arms. Not only was he huge in size, from his feet to his nose, but there was also an undercurrent of sensuality about him that in no way could be called deliberate. It was simply there . . . its force as overwhelming as the visible features that set him apart from any other man she knew.

"Er . . . I'm Shena McLean," she ventured rather hesitantly. They would have to exchange names sooner or later, she thought grimly, imagining how her insurance rates would soar.

"Ahh yes," he drawled flatly, "my neighbor." He made it sound like an accusation. "I'm Max Cramer, Miss McLean. I sincerely hope this isn't an example of how you normally drive, or else we're in for a long summer."

14

Shena searched his hard face for the tiniest glimmer of humor. Finding none, she asked the obvious. "Did I hear you say something about our being neighbors, Mr. Cramer?"

"You are *the* Shena McLean who owns the cabin back there, aren't you"—he indicated with a quick nod of his head—"the one being repaired?"

"Yes I am," Shena said quickly. "Don't tell me you are the mysterious owner of the one next to me."

"Unfortunately I am," he admitted, not at all pleased.

Not only are you ugly as sin, Shena thought nastily as she stared at him, you're also an insensitive clod. To her dismay she found she was not feeling sorry in the least for having nearly destroyed his car.

"Are you planning on staying in the area indefinitely or will you be using the cabin for a few weeks in the summer?" Please let it be the latter, she silently prayed. She had worked too long and too hard getting her place livable to have her peace and quiet ruined by a big-nosed, shaggy-haired, nasty-tempered brute.

"Do I detect a note of desperation in your voice that my answer to the first part of your question be no and a definite yes to the last?" he asked, and for the first time there was a hint of amusement in his eyes.

"I'm really not concerned one way or the other," she lied. "It's just that being this far from town, it

15

would be nice to know if I'm to have a full-time or an occasional neighbor."

"When I decide, I'll let you know," Max said shortly, his amber gaze making its way over Shena's petite figure with a slow mockery that set her teeth on edge. "In the meantime, I suggest we see about getting at least one of these vehicles running. This sudden stop in the rain isn't going to last for very long." And as though the heavens were adding emphasis to his dark prediction, there was a loud clap of thunder and a zigzagging bolt of lightning that caused Shena to jump at least an inch off the ground.

She cast a nervous look at the sky, then hastily followed her unpleasant neighbor through the brush.

What rotten luck, she frowned as she sought to match her stride to "Bigfoot's" by stepping into each damp track left by his large tread. She had hoped, someday, to be able to buy the cabin next to hers. It was a pipe dream, she admitted, but a dream nevertheless. She'd even gone so far as to try to locate the owner, but no one seemed to know who the owner was. Well, now she knew, and what a disappointment.

It didn't take more than a quick glance at the truck for her to know that nothing short of a miracle could bring that poor, tired thing back to life.

"I'm curious," Max Cramer mused, one large hand reaching up to rub at his chin as he stared with disbelief at the pickup. "Why on earth were you driving like a bat out of hell in this trap? Didn't you realize how dangerous it was?"

"I was in a hurry," Shena began to explain. "The engine—or some other thingamajig—was beginning to make some very odd sounds. I decided if it was going to tear up on me, I might as well get as far as I could . . . as fast as I could."

"Ahh, the thingamajig," he repeated with a smirk. "Well now, you certainly accomplished what you set out to do, didn't you?" he remarked dryly. He began to pick several pieces of the lumber off the ground and return them to the body of the pickup.

Shena bristled. She wasn't accustomed to being treated like such an incompetent. She ran her own business, a small landscape-nursery, and ran it quite successfully at that. Since her grandfather's death eight years ago she had been on her own. His legacy to her had been the run-down cabin and the full knowledge of his love for her. The goals she'd set for herself during those years had, for the most part, been reached. If the methods by which she managed her business and her day-to-day life seemed unorthodox to some people, then that was too bad. It suited her to a tee, and she had enough of her grandfather's Irish stubbornness to disregard whatever malcontents there were dotting her world.

After taking care of the lumber, the insufferable idiot she'd had the misfortune to run into turned his attention to his car. Shena stood back, resentful of his manner. He either ignored her or spoke to her in tones reminiscent of the Arctic. There were a number of questions she was dying to ask this tall, scowling man, but she didn't have quite enough nerve to brave the harshness of his gaze.

"If I lift the back bumper and push at the same time, I think it can be done," he said, thinking out loud. He went down on one knee, with his head almost touching the ground, while he peered underneath the rear of the car. After several moments, he rose to his feet, studying the situation.

He turned his shaggy head toward Shena with eyes that plainly revealed his irritation. "Well? Do you think you can do something so simple as start the car without running me down?"

Shena knew exactly what he had in mind to free his car of the mud. A monkey could do it . . . with its eyes closed. She opened her mouth to haughtily assure him that she was quite capable of performing such a simple task. But some perverse imp of mischief sitting on her shoulder brought an entirely different answer to her lips.

"Gee, Mr. Cramer," she replied innocently, taking on the vague look of a complete featherhead, "I'll do my best. I do hope your car isn't one of those complicated ones."

Max stared at her for several seconds, then shook his head with a rough grunt of annoyance. "All that will be necessary, Miss McLean, is for you to get in the car, start the engine and place your foot on the gas pedal. When you hear me yell 'Go,' you will press

18

on the pedal in hopes that with my combined efforts and your driving skill, which I find sadly lacking, we can successfully free my car from the mud." He straightened to his formidable height and looked down his huge, haughty nose at her. "Do you think you can keep all of those very complicated facts straight in your mind?"

"I'll try." Shena smiled brightly. She took a couple of steps toward the car, then stopped and looked back at him. "Should I put the gear whatchamacallit into reverse or neutral?"

She could barely contain her laughter when she saw his hands open, the fingers spread wide apart, his wrists stiff with controlled rage. It took a moment or two for the look of murderous intent to become masked with an expression of rigid control.

"Miss McLean," he said in a tight voice. "Please, once you've started the car and have heard my signal, place the gear selector in the drive position. Okay?" At her nod, he whirled around and savagely kicked a large pine cone several yards up the road.

Not wanting to push her luck, Shena worked her way around the car and climbed into the driver's seat. She reached for the key, turned it and heard the engine purr to life. Almost immediately she heard the word "Go!" She eased the gear selector into position, her foot moving instinctively toward the accelerator. But instead of the feel of the narrow rubber-covered pedal she was seeking, she found nothing but air.

19

She looked down and saw the object of her search a good two feet beyond the tip of her toe. "Cute," Shena muttered beneath her breath. "Real cute. Most people get involved with normal-sized people. Me? . . . I have to find an oversized jackass with a three-inch burr under his saddle."

With a disgusted toss of her auburn head, she reached over to roll down the window. Before she could do so, however, she heard another explosive "Go!"

Shena looked helplessly at the space between her foot and the accelerator. Her short acquaintance with Max Cramer left her in little doubt of his displeasure if she didn't comply with his explicit instructions. She heard his loud voice bellow, "I said go, dammit!"

Without further urging, Shena slid forward till her slender hips were directly beneath the steering wheel, the tip of her head barely visible through the windshield. She jammed her foot on the accelerator. The sound of the racing engine filled her ears and she felt the car jerk and move forward an inch or two. She knew the importance of keeping steady pressure on the pedal, but the awkwardness of her position caused her foot to slip. In that brief moment the car rolled back to its original position. Without hesitating, Shena rammed the accelerator again, the whine of the spinning back tires sounding shrill and eerie over the roar of the engine.

The car inched forward . . . one foot . . . another . . . another, till the tilted nose of the car, slowly leveled off. A huge sigh of relief escaped Shena as she found the brake and brought the vehicle to a stop. Before she had time to commend herself for a job well done, though, the car door was flung open. She found herself face-to-face with a most remarkable sight.

Her mouth dropped open, her lips forming a perfect O, as she met Max Cramer's mud-splattered face. But the damage didn't stop at his face, Shena realized, as the same calm came over her that comes when the eye of a hurricane is upon one. He looked for all the world as though someone had emersed his entire body in a huge drum filled with the dark ooze from the ditch on either side of the road.

Guiltily, she wiggled and squirmed away till the back of the seat stopped her retreat. The wild-eyed creature hovering over her was angry, was beside himself with anger, as she could see in the bone-crushing grip of his hands on the car door and the involuntary trembling of his long arms.

With a great deal of effort, Shena closed her mouth. Lord! She swallowed nervously as she swiftly reviewed her handiwork. She hadn't meant to do such a thorough job.

"Are you proud of yourself, Miss McLean?" The question was put to her like the flicking end of a rawhide whip.

"Er—I—I'm really sorry this happened to you, Mr. Cramer," she finally managed to spit out.

"Lady, if you were a man"—he paused, his head tipped forward at a menacing angle—"if you were even the size of a normal woman, I would drag you out of that car and beat the flaming hell out of you. You"—he jerked one hand away from the door long enough to shake a long, mud-covered forefinger in her face—"are a one-man demolition expert . . . a blight, a curse upon normal human beings. Trouble follows you like fleas on a dog. If they still burned witches at the stake, you'd be at the top of the list."

"Well—well really, Mr. Cramer." Shena tried to defend herself the moment he gulped for air. "I was only following your instructions. How was I to know that you'd slipped and fallen? And another thing, I may be small, but it beats the hell out of being the size of a water buffalo. If your front seat hadn't been in the backseat I might have been able to have more control over the situation."

"Control, hell!" Max shouted. "Did the position of the seat cause you to go stone deaf? Did it cause your eyesight to suddenly go bad? I yelled my lungs out for you to stop. But no"—he gave a mirthless snort—"not you. You had your damned foot pressed so hard on that accelerator it's a wonder you aren't circling the moon by now with me flying out behind like the damn tail on a kite. I surrendered after swallowing the first five pounds of mud. But did you bother to look around and see if all was well? No, not Miss Give'm Hell McLain."

"Mr. Cramer"—Shena looked him straight in the

22

eye, her voice deadly calm—"please do me a favor. Go straight to hell." Without another word, she slid to the other side of the car and got out. She rounded the front, her angry gaze set on the truck. But something in the rude, arrogant way he had treated her made her stop and turn toward him. "You are without a doubt the meanest, the most insensitive clod I've ever met. I apologized for hitting your car and I did my best to help you. But instead of accepting my apology and making the most out of a bad situation, you became a wild, ranting moron. I think you should seriously consider selling your cabin, for I doubt the two of us will be able to live that close without one of us shooting the other."

Shena carried a glass of lemonade in one hand as she slowly walked through the four rooms of the small cabin, the ends of her hair still damp from her shower. It had taken a shower, a long one, to calm her down after her encounter with her neighbor. But at the moment a smile of outright contentment covered the delicate structure of her face as she stopped and touched the rough-hewn smoothness of a log wall. The sound of Win's hammering filled the background. Not even the forbidding thought of Max Cramer lurking next door could take away the happiness she felt as she surveyed her small kingdom.

It had taken her over a year to get this far. Long months of penny-pinching, of working evenings and most weekends. Friends had lent time and effort to her project of renovating the small rustic cabin. The only paid employee had been a carpenter who specialized in restoring old houses. Shena had hired him to complete the more structural remodeling. Since then, she and Win had worked at finishing the job whenever they had a spare moment.

From her position in the door of the living room, she could see most of the kitchen and small patches of each bedroom. Over the last few weeks several pieces of furniture had begun to fill the empty rooms, things that had been in storage and a number of boxes from Shena's apartment. If everything went as planned, she would move in permanently by the first of the month. And since that was only five days away, she reminded herself, she'd better get cracking.

"Shena!" Win yelled at the top of his voice, shattering her peaceful reverie. "Where have you hidden the nails?"

"I haven't touched them," she answered in a disgusted voice. She walked to the doorway of the small bedroom and stared at Win. "Why is it that every time you can't find something, you automatically think I've hidden it from you?"

Win gave her a quick glance from his perch on the stepladder, then continued measuring and marking. "Because you were born with a neatness fetish," he told her as he scribbled on a block of wood. "Ferreting things out of sight is a way of life with you just the same as eating is with most people. But if you don't

24

leave the tools and all the other things I need to work with alone, I'm going to choke you."

"I'm petrified." Shena stuck out her tongue at him, then began searching among the several boxes sitting on the floor in one corner of the room. She unearthed the particular box of nails she knew he wanted, then walked over and handed them to him.

"Have you heard from 'Handsome Kip'?" he asked as he bent down to retrieve the nails.

"The answer to that question is the same as it was yesterday and the day before . . . and the day before that." Shena glared at him. "You know Kip isn't one for doing a lot of calling or writing when he goes out of town."

"How understanding," Win hooted derisively. "Poor Kip is so busy he can't even take time out for a lousy three-minute telephone call. God!" He shook his head. "I can't believe how that two-timing creep has all you gals believing these incredible tales."

"Jealous, Win?" Shena taunted.

"Unfortunately, kiddo, there's nothing to be jealous of. The only time I think of Kip Harris is in connection with you. You've been dating him off and on for well over a year now. Don't you know when you're facing a losing battle?"

"Who appointed you 'Dear Abby' of Willow Creek?" She frowned. He had a point, dammit, but she could see things in Kip that Win and several other of their mutual friends seemed unaware of.

He was sensitive, caring, handsome and he needed

her. "You're so easy to talk to, Shena," he'd told her on more than one occasion. Shena's heart had swelled with pride as she sat and listened to him relate the pressures of his profession. He needed her! She had hung on to that thought for days afterward. Still, she had to admit that Win's tiny jabs had hit home. Kip didn't call or write when he was away on business . . . and that annoyed her. Lately there had been other little things about him that had bothered her. Things so insignificant as to make her appear foolish for mentioning them, but bothersome just the same.

All through high school Shena had cherished a "burning passion" for Kip Harris, blushing like crazy when the handsome senior would turn his flashing smile upon her, a lowly sophomore. Fortunately, college and maturity had gone a long way toward equalizing the situation. Now she was beginning to find herself in the rather uncomfortable position of continuously having to defend Kip. Strange, she thought as she stared out the window toward the cabin next door. She never realized just how unpopular he was with their friends, with people they'd both grown up with.

Suddenly there was such an ungodly clatter out front, Shena nearly jumped out of her skin. She turned and hurried toward the front door, a curious Win climbing down from the ladder and following directly behind her. But instead of some automobile having smashed through one of the cabin walls, or some other such catastrophe, they found a scowling Max Cramer and another equally unpleasant-looking man unloading the lumber Shena had left on the truck.

CHAPTER TWO

"Who on earth is that?" Win asked in a whisper as he observed the two men taking the lumber from the rear of a Ford Bronco.

"My new neighbor," Shena informed him. "At least that big mean-looking, shaggy-haired one is. I haven't as yet met his hatchet-faced friend."

Win turned and stared at her, his blue eyes practically bulging from their sockets. "Are you telling me that's the man you ran off the road?"

"Yes!" she snapped. "Why the shocked expression? Would you rather I'd gone after some little old nun in a wheelchair?" she asked icily.

"Yes!" he answered with equal spirit. "That character looks mean enough to burn your house down just for the hell of it. There's no telling what he might do now that you've ruined his car."

Shena had no answer for Win's gloomy prediction and, even if she had, it would have stuck in her throat. For at that moment Max Cramer dropped the last piece of lumber on the neatly stacked pile and turned toward the front door of the cabin.

Shena was suddenly covered with goose bumps as she forced herself to step out onto the porch. She quelled her almost uncontrollable urge to run as she watched the long, clean strides of her neighbor eating up the distance separating them. Though he'd obviously taken a bath since his encounter with the mud, the shirt he was now wearing was damp with perspiration and had a small tear in one sleeve. His dark pants had been replaced by a pair of faded, tattered jeans. She wondered fleetingly if she should offer to wash the clothes that had been ruined, then just as quickly discarded the idea. With her luck where he was concerned, her washing machine would probably turn into a monster and eat each garment down to the last thread.

He paused when he reached the edge of the porch. One large foot was placed on the edge and he leaned forward, bracing his forearms across his raised thigh, his gaze pinned on Shena.

"Since your truck is out of commission, we thought it might be a good idea to pick up your lumber. I hope we put the wood where you wanted it," he said, breaking the paralysis holding Shena in its grip.

"Th-that's fine, Mr. Cramer, thank you," she politely replied. "And in case you're wondering, I checked with my insurance agent and he assured me there would be no problem with your car."

He shrugged. "I'll get around to it in a couple of days. There's still the problem of your truck. Do you have some way of towing it into town?" he asked. As he spoke his gaze made a slow but thorough study of Shena's small body.

She found herself unable to concentrate on the question of her truck, wishing instead that she were wearing a floor-length gingham dress with a collar that went all the way to her chin rather than the white shorts and green halter. Damn the man! Even his gaze set her teeth on edge. "I think I can manage to have the truck moved," she said coolly. "There's a scrap-metal dealer in town who will probably pick it up for me."

"Don't worry about the truck, Shena," Win spoke up as he came out onto the porch. "I'll have someone take care of it for you." He walked toward the male visitor and extended his hand. "I'm Win Logan."

"Max Cramer," came the raspy reply. After exchanging a brief handshake, Max gave Win an assessing look. "Winfield," he said thoughtfully. "Are you related to the Winfield that's president of one of the local banks?"

" 'Fraid so," the affable Win replied. "He's my father. Do you know him?"

"Vaguely." Max shrugged off the answer. He stared at the carpenter's apron Win was wearing and the flat pencil behind his ear. "Are you a carpenter?"

"Only on weekends," Win laughed. "Several of us have been lending Shena a hand with the renovation of this place. And"—he looked about proudly—"if I do say so myself, I think we've done a very nice job.

As a matter of fact, if you're interested, I'd be happy to show you around."

"Really, Win," Shena spoke up. "I'm sure Mr. Cramer isn't interested in what we're doing." At least I hope he isn't, she thought grimly. She didn't want this odious person parading through her home. Besides that, he might decide to sit down, and she wasn't certain she had a single chair that would withstand his weight.

"How kind of you to offer me an easy way out, Miss McLean," Max said snidely. "However, I can't think of any pressing business at the moment." He reached out and grasped one of the supporting posts and drew himself up onto the porch. "Shall we get the tour under way?"

"Do you think your friend's interested?" Win asked, nodding toward the taciturn man who was leaning against the four-wheel-drive vehicle.

"I doubt it," Max said shortly. "Fred doesn't care much for people or looking at renovated cabins."

If looks could have killed, Shena was certain both men would have fallen stone dead at her feet. "In that case, I'll leave you in Win's capable hands," she snapped. Casting one last stinging glance at Win, she turned on her heel and hurried inside the house, not stopping till she reached the kitchen. There were several large boxes waiting to be unpacked. She flipped open the cover of one, then plunged into it with both hands, tossing aside the newspaper and banging kitchen utensils onto the counter.

By the time Win and "his" guest had worked their way through the interior of the cabin and were entering the kitchen, Shena had managed to work off some of her anger toward both men. She was bent over the tall sides of the packing box, her head, arms and a good portion of her upper body buried in the cardboard confines. She was struggling to lift a set of stainless-steel mixing bowls.

Suddenly two large tanned hands grasped her upper arms and lifted her, mixing bowls and all, upright. "Couldn't you have found a shorter box?" Max Cramer asked. He took the mixing bowls from her unresisting fingers and plunked them down on the counter. Then he peered into the box as though to reassure himself that it was empty.

Shena gathered her dignity about her like a small ruffled hen and glared at him. "I prefer to use larger packing containers. They hold more."

"They're also impossible for someone your size to unpack," the scruffy, unkempt giant informed her.

"Ahh, but you don't know my Shena," Win joined the conversation. "When she makes up her mind to do something, hell or high water won't change her course." He dropped a casual arm across Shena's shoulders and gave her a brief hug. "I sure wish you'd listen to the man, Shena. Moving those heavy things around is too much for you."

Shena knew that what they were saying was true. She cursed herself each time she unloaded one of the large boxes. But nothing short of being stretched on

32

the rack and having hot pokers of steel pressed against the soles of her feet could have wrung such an admission from her.

She turned her face up to Win's and gave him such a sickeningly sweet smile that his mouth dropped open. "But that's what I have you around for, isn't it, sweetie?"

"Not me," he said flatly, wondering if a bump on the head when she'd wrecked the truck was responsible for her strange behavior. "I detest unpacking. Are you sure you're all right, Shena?" he asked worriedly.

The corners of her small mouth turned down with annoyance. There was no doubt about it, men had to be the most stupid creatures on God's green earth. "Of course I'm all right," she snapped at him. Then she turned her attention to Max Cramer, who was leaning against the counter, his arms crossed over his chest, watching them.

"Well, Mr. Cramer, what do you think of our efforts?"

"It's very nice, Miss McLean," he said sincerely. "Will you be living by yourself when you move in?" It was an innocent enough question on the surface but Shena caught the hint of mockery in his voice. He hadn't been at all fooled by her little performance with Win!

Nothing would have suited her better than to tell him that Win would be living with her, even if Win *did* think her completely nuts. But she couldn't go that far. Instead she said, "I'll be living on my own, Mr. Cramer. For the time being, at least."

"I've been thinking about that." Win frowned. "You'll be rather cut off from things out here," he said thoughtfully. "But now that Mr. Cramer is next door you shouldn't feel frightened. And you know you can call me anytime you're scared. I won't mind coming out and spending the occasional night with you."

Some help he was! Only a fool would refuse to accept defeat when it was staring her in the face, Shena decided, and she certainly wasn't a fool. Win was not going to help her in her little game. "That's what makes you so special, Win." She smiled sweetly. "I know I can always depend on you to solve all my problems for me. By the way," she remarked as she turned to start unpacking another box, "did you show Mr. Cramer the deck we've started?"

"Since we're going to be neighbors, why don't we drop the Mr. and Miss business?" Max inserted smoothly, the glint of amusement in his amber eyes letting Shena know that he wasn't fooled in the least by her antics.

"Sounds great," Win enthused expansively, unaware of the undercurrents of animosity between Max and Shena. "The deck's just out this door, Max." And to Shena's relief, the two of them disappeared from the kitchen.

Several hours later, with every bone in her body aching and her face smeared with newsprint, Shena

34

stepped back to look with pride at what she'd accomplished in her afternoon's work.

The cupboard shelves had been lined with a tiny blue-and-white-flowered paper and were now filled with dishes and food. There were crisp, ruffled white curtains at the windows, tied back with light blue ribbons. Baskets of different shapes and in a variety of earth tones hung from the open-beamed ceiling. Potted geraniums of bright coral adorned both window ledges. The shine of the slate flooring and the gleam of the copper kettle on the stove lent warmth to the room and gave it that certain country touch Shena was seeking.

"Patting yourself on the back?" Win asked as he entered the room and headed for the sink.

"Sort of," Shena admitted. "I've carried the picture of this room in my mind for so long, it's difficult for me to believe that I'm really seeing it now."

"Well, enjoy it, squirt." He threw her a huge grin over his sawdust-covered shoulder. "You've worked hard enough for it."

"Oh I will enjoy it, believe me. I . . . What on earth are you doing?" she cried in disbelief. She flew across to the sink and stared with horror at the paint-spattered mess he'd made.

"I'm washing out this paint brush. What's eating you anyway? You've been acting strange all afternoon."

"You're making an unholy mess in my new sink, that's what's eating me!" Shena yelled at him.

"Couldn't you have used the faucet out back for that?"

"I suppose I could have, but I didn't think of it. Sorry." Win grinned. Before she knew what he was up to, he reached out and drew a blue line down each side of her face with the tip of his finger. "Now you're perfectly coordinated with the antique chest in your guest bedroom."

"How sweet," Shena muttered crossly. She opened the cupboard beneath the sink and removed a sponge and a can of cleanser, then thrust both articles into his hands. "Now you can become 'perfectly' acquainted with the sink."

Without quibbling, Win set to cleaning up the mess he'd made. "Would you mind telling me what you were trying to prove when Max Cramer was here? And in case you don't remember, I'll refresh your memory." He let his head drop back onto his shoulders and fluttered his lashes like a 1930s movie queen. "That's what I have you around for, isn't it, sweetie?" he drawled in a syrupy voice.

"Well if you weren't so thickheaded, you'd have guessed by now why I did it." Shena tried to sound angry. "We don't know a darn thing about Max Cramer. Doesn't it strike you as odd that he told us nothing about himself, but bombarded us with questions the entire time he was here? And another thing, when we had our accident earlier, he already knew my name."

"So?"

"So I don't like the idea of being alone with that ill-tempered brute prowling about. His friend Fred doesn't look to be any friendlier."

"I suppose you do have a point," Win conceded. "I'll see what Dad knows about him. Will that make you feel any better?"

"I suppose so. What really aggravates me though is the fact that he sneaked in and bought the cabin. You know I've had my eye on that place for ages."

"Now you're being childish, honey," Win said without hesitation. "You've plowed every penny you can scrape together to get this place fixed up and to keep your business going."

"But as my financial adviser it's your job to find ways for me to carry out my fantasies." Shena grinned.

"Fulfilling your fantasies would require the dedication of a miracle worker," he countered wickedly. "You're working much too hard as it is. Speaking of work, now that you've wrecked the truck, what will you do for transportation when your van is tied up?"

"That's a problem I'm trying not to think about until Monday morning. Do you have any ideas?" she asked hopefully.

"Maybe I do. I'll see what I can come up with."

The weekend would have been perfect, Shena thought as she drove to work on Monday morning, if it hadn't been for Max Cramer always hanging in the shadows. Not that he'd deliberately intruded in any

37

way, she sighed. But each time she'd happened to glance toward his place, he'd managed to come into her line of vision.

She found herself wondering what line of work he was in. It must be a lucrative one, whatever it was. In only a matter of hours he had come up with a new vehicle after the accident. And on Saturday another dark Lincoln had materialized in front of his house.

There hadn't been any sign of a woman during the weekend nor had she heard any reference to a wife. Shena found herself speculating on what sort of woman it would take to make a man like Max Cramer happy, then quickly scolded herself for letting her thoughts go completely haywire.

Yet, as difficult as it was for her to admit, there was something about the grouchy wretch that was appealing. Appealing and at the same time intimidating. She'd been aware of it that first moment in the rain when she turned and stared at him in the opened door of the truck. That appeal, that magnetism, had struck her like some invisible force, as powerful a facet of his personality as the anger he'd shown. He was unlike any man she had ever known.

Whatever brief moments of relaxation Shena had been able to find over the weekend were soon forgotten when she went back to work Monday. By the time she'd opened the shop and had got through the first two hours of the new day, the weekend seemed far behind her.

At the nursery the first thing to catch her eye as she

went to turn on the sprinkler was the shipment of gardenias that Charlie had accepted on Friday afternoon. Even an untrained eye could see the thousands of tiny white flies clinging to the dark green leaves.

"Damn!" she muttered with disgust, turning to the shed where the insecticides and sprayers were kept. The gardenias would have to be moved to the back and sprayed. Then she would have to wait for at least six weeks before they could be sold.

"I've been told that talking to yourself is a sure-fire sign that you are about to crack up," Chloe Jackson, Shena's one full-time employee, remarked wryly as she fell into step beside her boss. "What's Charlie done now?"

"Why does it have to be Charlie?" Shena sighed. "It could be something you've done."

"No." Chloe gave a decisive shake of her dark head. "I'm very competent. Charlie, on the other hand, is a complete air-head. I don't know why you put up with him."

"Mainly because he's willing to work for practically nothing."

"And?"

"And . . . I suppose I like him. He's working his tail off trying to get through school."

"Then let's hope that someday, when he's made fortune ripping off sick people, he'll bail you out of the certain bankruptcy you're headed for if you continue to let him work here."

"Point taken, Chloe," Shena said, hoping to ward off a lengthy lecture.

"Where do you want to put the gardenias?"

"Ahh . . . you noticed?"

"How could I not? Every time I brush by them a white cloud lifts up like Geronimo sending out smoke signals."

Shena chuckled, then turned to the unpleasant task at hand.

Business was brisk all morning, leaving Shena little time to work on an order she needed to place with several wholesalers. It was well into the afternoon before she was able to escape to her small office and get started on the paperwork.

She'd been at her desk only a short while when Win called. "How's business?" he asked pleasantly.

"Rather busy for a Monday."

"Well, I hope you can get away, because I think I've found a car to replace your old pickup. And what's more, I think it's one you can afford."

"Er . . . how affordable is it?" Shena asked cautiously. "It can't be much of a car if it's in my price range."

"True," Win agreed. "But then it beats the heck out of a bicycle." He named a figure that even Shena had to agree was reasonable.

"Are you sure it runs?"

"It runs, and reasonably well for its age, I might add. It's part of an estate the bank has recently settled."

"You mean it really did belong to a little old lady?"
Shena laughed.

"No, it was a little old man. And as far as anyone
can remember, he only drove to town and back twice
a week. The car needs a paint job, but other than
that, it's not bad. Can you break loose for thirty minutes or so?"

Shena agreed to meet him. Setting her work aside,
she went off in search of Chloe.

"A little old man drove this?" Shena asked incredulously some time later as she slowly walked around
the strangest-colored little Volkswagen she'd ever
seen. "It looks like it's suffered through a severe case
of the measles."

"Never mind what it looks like," Win told her.
"The engine is still in good condition and it will be
economical on gas." He looked enormously pleased
with himself. "What more could you ask for?"

"What more indeed," Shena chuckled. "But are
you sure the bank will finance it for me?"

"I'm positive we will. In fact, the paperwork is on
my desk waiting for your signature." He handed her
the keys. "Would you like to drive it back?"

Shena's elation was short-lived, however, when she
found herself in the driver's seat. Her van had an
automatic transmission and so had the pickup. This
car had a gear stick on the floor, which Shena hated.
But considering that she would never find another
car for such a low price, and after all the trouble Win

41

had gone to on her behalf, she gritted her teeth and turned the key. Lack of money certainly enabled one a variety of new adventures, she thought grimly, her forward progress a series of starts and jumps.

Back at the nursery, Chloe and Charlie took turns walking around the strange-looking little car, their expressions a mixture of disbelief and disgust.

"What color was it originally?" Chloe finally asked after the fourth or fifth trip around.

"It's not so bad," Charlie assured her. "In fact"—he scratched at his ear with one finger, his head tilted at an angle—"the longer you look at it, the more it grows on you." He looked at Shena and grinned. "I like it."

"You would," Chloe hooted.

"I think I agree with you, Charlie, I like it too," she said quickly, hoping to prevent a battle in the parking lot. "Do either of you need a lift?"

"Are you kidding?" Chloe laughed.

"No thanks, I got my bike fixed," Charlie said quickly. "See ya tomorrow." He waved, then loped over to a wicked-looking motorbike. Shena smiled after him as she watched him roar out of the parking lot.

She quickly followed suit and was soon at her apartment, where she changed into a pair of faded jeans and an old T-shirt. Then she began loading a few remaining boxes into the car, readying for her trip to the cabin.

Apparently something as frivolous as air-condition-ing in a car had been a no-no to the previous owner of the car, Shena decided as she drove through town and turned onto the interstate, the wind from the open window blowing her hair into wild disarray. But despite the snail's pace she was traveling at and her dread at the thought of shifting gears, the gleam of enthusiasm sparkling in her blue eyes remained.

The cabin had become her haven, the one place in her life that wasn't overrun with harassed housewives or bleary-eyed husbands making war on crab grass or griping because the shrubs they'd planted in the middle of summer were looking droopy.

When the dirt road leading to the cabin came into view, Shena placed her left foot on the clutch and pressed down, intending to shift into first gear. But instead of going into place smoothly, as it was supposed to, the wretched lever seemed to have a mind of its own and stubbornly refused to move out of neutral.

With its frustrated driver trying to manage the brake, the clutch and to shift at the same time, the car came to a complete stop. Unfortunately, Shena's humiliation wasn't over. The moment she took her foot off the brake, the strange little car began rolling backward.

"This can't be happening," Shena muttered furiously as she jammed her foot on the brake. After several hectic moments of tugging and trying to force the gear lever into place, she dropped back against the seat and closed her eyes, wiping at the tiny rivulets of perspiration that were trickling down her face and neck.

Suddenly, a voice appeared out of nowhere.

"I'm sure you'll have a perfectly logical explanation, and I'll probably hate myself for asking, but would you mind telling me why you've chosen to park smack in the middle of the road? Are you ill?"

Shena shot forward like the volley from a cannon, her head spinning around, her startled eyes focusing on Max Cramer's disturbing features. He was standing beside the car, quietly watching her as though doubtful of her sanity.

A number of curt remarks rushed front and center to her mind, particularly one about expensive cars that allowed their owners to sneak up on unsuspecting people. Oddly enough, though, she found herself not wanting to fight. She was hot, she was tired and not nearly mad enough to hold her own in an argument with Max Cramer.

She raised her arms and rested them on the steering wheel. "It's the gear lever," she began, then went on to explain what had happened. "So, since I can't get it out of neutral, and being on this hill, my only recourse is to let the car roll backward till I can get it off the road."

Max stepped back from the VW. He let his thoughtful gaze travel over the boxes crammed into the front and back seats, then he looked at Shena as he pondered her problem. "Well," he finally spoke, "I think the best thing to do is tow you to the cabin.

44

After that I'll take a look and see what the problem is. How does that sound?"

"Wh-why it sounds fine," Shena stammered. Help from Max Cramer? That was the last thing she expected from him. "There's just one problem, Mr. . . . er, Max. I've never been towed before. What am I supposed to do?"

Max threw up both hands in a halting gesture. "Nothing," he quickly assured her. "All you have to do is steer and make sure you don't ram the rear of my car when we turn and when we reach the cabin. Think you can handle that?"

"Lord, I hope so." Shena sighed. "If I have another accident claim, my insurance agent will kill me." She grasped the steering wheel firmly with both hands. "Well, let's get started."

Amusement and a healthy look of respect were mirrored in Max's gaze as he watched her unconsciously square her slim shoulders and take a deep breath. Without thinking, he reached inside the car with one hand and let the tips of his fingers lightly trail the fragile line of her cheek. "Don't look so grim," he said softly. "If you do happen to mess up, I'll see to the claim. Intimidating suspicious insurance agents is something I do quite well. But there is one thing that puzzles me."

"What's that?" Shena asked in a not so steady voice. The touch of his hand on her face had left her with a tingling sensation streaking throughout her

45

body. It had been unexpected, strangely upsetting and remarkably pleasant.

"Where do you manage to find these unbelievable vehicles you keep coming up with?"

CHAPTER THREE

Shena kept her eyes glued to the rear end of the Lincoln ahead of her as though her very life depended on not marring its surface. Which it probably does, she thought fleetingly as moments later the two cabins came into view. Max Cramer had appeared to be friendly enough today, she grudgingly admitted, but she wasn't at all taken in by his docile mood. She seriously doubted he would remain calm if she were to ram the VW into the elegantly designed rear of this second Lincoln.

A huge sigh of relief escaped her as the last few yards of the journey were completed. Shena pressed her foot on the brake and switched off the ignition. She remained perfectly still as she watched Max get out of his car and walk back to her. Then he opened the door on the driver's side.

The sight of her grim features and her hands gripping the steering wheel brought the closest thing to a smile she'd seen from him to Max's lips. "You can relax now," he told her. "The worst is over."

"I wouldn't be so sure about that if I were you,"

Shena replied. "In my brief acquaintance with this car, I've come to realize one important thing—it has a mind of its own."

He chuckled, and Shena was not only amazed at the sound, she liked it. "Is something wrong?" he asked, seeing the glint of surprise in her blue eyes.

"You laughed," she blurted out, then rushed on before she lost her nerve. "That's the first human thing I've seen you do since we met. You should do it more often, it's a remarkable improvement."

Max bent forward and rested his wide hands on the roof of the small car, the swiftness of the move bringing his face uncomfortably close to hers. "Is it a habit of yours to try and correct the personality quirks of all the people you meet?" he asked in such a soft voice Shena felt the hair on her neck standing on end.

"Er . . . no, of course not," she stammered, intrigued by the strength and power of his incredible face with its hodgepodge features.

"Then why pick on me?" Max continued his quiet taunting, his amber eyes darting about her face with open curiosity.

Shena swallowed, hoping to dispel the nervousness his nearness had brought. "I—I just thought you should know," she murmured inanely. "After all, we are going to be neighbors."

"Ahh." He almost smiled. "True neighborly concern." His warm breath brushed her flaming cheeks.

"Does that mean that you no longer resent the fact that I live next door?"

"Well," Shena sighed, wishing she were any place else in the world than inches from Max Cramer, "Well, I wouldn't go that far." She turned her head and stared at the cabin he'd bought, regret bringing a rueful lift to her shoulders. "I've had my eye on that cabin ever since it became vacant two years ago."

"Unfortunately, speculating in real estate can have its disappointing moments. Not to mention that it's an expensive undertaking," said Max.

"True," Shena reluctantly agreed. "But human nature being what it is, it's always easier to feel anger at another person for destroying your dream than it is to face reality, don't you agree?" She blushed suddenly, surprised at her candid words. There was nothing in their relationship to warrant an exchange of philosophies. "Thank you, Max, for helping me with the car," she added quickly. "If you hadn't come along I'd probably still be sitting on the road."

"No problem," he said easily, pushing himself upright and stepping back so that she could get out. "Do you want any help with those boxes?"

"Oh no." Shena shook her head. "You've done more than enough. I can manage. Thanks again." She smiled briefly, then turned and walked toward the cabin. It wasn't until she heard the sound of his car leaving that she let out a nervous sigh.

There was something infinitely disturbing about Max Cramer, she thought later as she trudged back

49

and forth between the cabin and the car, her arms straining against the weight of the boxes. Something dangerous as well—one smile from the ugly beast and she had started rambling on like a fool. The next time she saw Mr. Cramer, she thought the best thing she could do was place a piece of tape over her mouth.

Her resolution was all but forgotten when she opened her door a short while later to see what sneaky rat was trying to steal her car. It took only one look at the jean-clad figure leaning over the engine of her VW for Shena to discover the identity of the culprit.

She let the door slam, hurrying across the porch and down the steps. "What are you doing?" she demanded when she reached the car and saw the shambles he'd made out of the wires.

"What does it look like?" came the sharp retort.

"It looks like you're planning to give the junk dealer another piece of my property," she snapped back. "Has it occurred to you that I didn't ask for your help?" Damn his rude hide! Why couldn't he stay on his own property?

"It occurred to me," he said, straightening to his full height and turning to stare down at her, "right after I had the uncomfortable vision of having to fish you and this pile of junk out of the creek. Or having you come hurtling through the wall into my bedroom."

"I wouldn't be caught dead in your bedroom, you

50

ugly, ill-tempered beast!" Shena yelled at him, her small body fairly dancing with rage as she glowered at him.

Max picked up a faded rag and proceeded to wipe his hands, his gaze never leaving her. He ran one hand over his amused face and grinned. "Now you've hurt my feelings. Any number of your fair sex have told me that there's character etched in these noble features."

"Noble my—"

The sentence was abruptly cut off as Shena found herself plucked from the ground and crushed against the wall of muscle and bone of his bare chest. One steel-enforced arm clamped tightly around her waist with long square-tipped fingers splayed against her midriff. The other arm ran from her waist to her nape, the fingers of his hand cradling the back of her head.

Shena stared with wide-eyed amazement at the smiling mouth descending upon hers. She struggled wildly in her mind in that brief second for some way to stop it, but knew she was helpless to do so.

She felt the involuntary stiffening of her body as it prepared itself for the punishment about to ensue. Her thoughts went into high gear, calling to mind her fear of this man, as she desperately tried to think how she could defend herself. She wondered how the headlines in the newspaper woud read the next day when they fished her body from the creek.

And then the most unusual sensations began coursing her body. The terrifying fears of her imminent demise were being slowly pushed aside by the feel of gentle lips against hers and the exciting tip of a velvet tongue slowly tracing the outline of her mouth.

Shena felt herself drowning in a swirling whirlpool of excitement. The blood was surging wildly in her veins as Max's mouth began to brush back and forth across hers, teasing and tasting until she was clutching at his shoulders for support, her heart racing like crazy.

This isn't Kip, she told herself as she tried to capture his elusive lips. This isn't like anything I've ever known, she admitted. Tiring of Max's teasing, she reached up and grasped his great shaggy head and held it still. She opened her mouth to him, then heard the tiny groan that was her own voice as his tongue made whispery inroads into the mysterious sweetness welcoming him.

"Found a new way of working on brakes, Max?" asked a strange voice. Max raised his head and Shena stiffened, ready to die at being caught necking with a relative stranger.

"What do you want, Fred?" Max asked in a cool voice. His hand at the back of Shena's head kept her face pressed against his chest, his other arm still clamped around her body.

"There's a telephone call for you. Will you be tied up long?"

The question sent a red flush sweeping over Shena's face. The miserable fink! If she could only get loose from the caveman holding her, she'd show that detestable wimp a thing or two!

"Take their number, Fred. I'll be along later," Max instructed him. After a moment or two had passed, he eased back a step, letting his hands slide down Shena's arms before he slowly released her. "I'm sorry Fred embarrassed you, although I'm not the least bit sorry for kissing you." He reached out and allowed one finger to follow the wildly beating pulse in the side of her neck. "You're a very desirable woman, Shena McLean. Who taught you to kiss, Win Logan?"

My God! Shena thought dazedly, she must be in the throes of a dream. All her encounters with Max had been stimulating. His kiss, though, was devastating. As for her response, it was as much a shocker to her as it was to him.

"Win is a childhood friend, not my lover." She meant her reply to sound careless and flip, but it didn't. How could it, when she was still reeling from the touch of his hands on her body and the feel of his lips still warm on her mouth? Even the scent of him still clung to her.

Sensing the bleak frustration catching her in its web and the quiet panic building in her eyes, something snapped in Max, something so long forgotten that it's reawakening was like a blow to the midsection. Without hesitation, he placed his hands on Shena's shoulders and turned her around to face the cabin. "Go inside and finish unpacking your boxes, honey, I'll come back later and take care of the car."

It had been a cowardly escape, Shena later admitted as she emptied the last of the boxes, but a necessary one. Even now she could close her eyes and feel the quivering strength of him beneath her fingertips.

But what did she know about Max Cramer? she asked herself. Nothing. Not a single solitary thing. She picked up a stray sock and tucked it into a drawer, her brow furrowed as she tried to remember the tiniest thing he'd mentioned in their previous conversations. But they hadn't really talked. In fact, nothing about their relationship, if it could be called such, had run along the norm.

She closed her eyes against the thought of how easily she'd melted into his arms, dreading the moment when she would have to face him again. She wasn't some sixteen-year-old, she silently groaned, she was twenty-six, with a reasonable amount of experience. So why couldn't she shrug off this . . . this "encounter" . . . and act as though nothing had happened?

The sound of a car coming to a halt in front of the cabin gave her another reprieve, only this time it was from her muddled thoughts, not the root of her attraction for a man she barely knew.

She crossed over to the window and peeked out, then gave a gasp of surprise. Kip! On winged feet, she flew from the sparsely furnished guest bedroom and across the living room. She flung open the door and ran straight into the arms of the tall, tanned blond-headed man.

"Why didn't you let me know you were coming home?" she asked as soon as Kip stopped kissing her and set her back on her feet. "You've been gone for over a week and I've had nothing but one lousy phone call."

"I've been busy," he defended himself, giving her the crooked smile that always had her ready to believe his every word. This time, however, she was surprised to find herself wondering if he'd ever stood in front of a mirror and practiced that particular move? He had it down pat. "I did try to get you over the weekend, however, but you didn't answer your phone." He stepped around her and walked on into the room. He let his gaze move slowly over the finishing touches, completed since he'd been away. "Now I can see why. You've really been busy, haven't you?"

"Every available minute," she said proudly. She hooked an arm through his and smiled up at him. "What do you think of it?" she asked, pulling him along on a grand tour.

"It's great." Kip smiled lavishly. "But hey! I didn't come all the way out here just to look at the cabin. Have you had dinner? Wouldn't you like to get away from the crickets and the frogs for a while?"

"No, I haven't had dinner," Shena told him, masking her disappointment. "In fact, I'd forgotten all about it." Don't be hurt, she told herself a few minutes later as she showered and quickly dressed for dinner. Kip was . . . Kip. It wasn't fair to get mad at him simply because he wasn't as enthusiastic about the cabin as most of her friends were. He's good for me, she thought, trying to ignore the pang of resentment rearing its unpleasant head. He made her get out, made her forget the fact that she was up to her neck in debt and quite likely to stay that way for some time to come.

Her pep talk worked, and by the time she rejoined Kip, Shena had a smile on her lips and a lightness in her step. The one thing she couldn't control, however, as she walked beside him to his car, was the stubbornness of her gaze as it kept straying toward the next cabin and the outline of Max's silhouette on the front porch.

During the course of the evening, Shena sparkled. She smiled. She laughed at the proper moments and she listened. When friends stopped by their table at the restaurant and wanted to talk about the work on the cabin, she kept her progress reports to a minimum so as not to offend Kip. In short, she told herself as she sat listening to a lengthy list of *his* accomplishments during *his* latest trip, she felt like a fledgling actress trying out for a number of roles.

"Is something bothering you this evening, Shena?" Kip asked as soon as two friends left their table. "You aren't your usual sparkly self." He made it sound almost like an accusation, and Shena felt her temper rising.

"Well now, let's see," she looked straight across the

table at him, her blue gaze neither soft nor wavering. "I got to the shop around seven-thirty this morning, moved a shipment of gardenias and sprayed them, walked about ten miles during the course of the day, doing such mundane things as waiting on customers and loading numerous plants, carted several heavy boxes from the apartment down to my car, had car trouble on the way to the cabin, unloaded and unpacked the boxes once I did get there." She gave him a cool, brittle smile. "I suppose what's bothering me is simple. I'm tired. As a matter of fact, I'm ready to go home."

"Well really, Shena," Kip curtly replied. "You could have told me earlier. I'd planned on us stopping by my apartment and having a drink."

"I was delighted that you surprised me, Kip, and dinner was wonderful." She attempted to soothe him. "But I'm afraid the drink is out of the question."

"Now you're ready to go back to the woods again and resume the 'country gal' routine." He frowned, signaling the waiter for the check, his mouth drawn in an uncompromising line across his handsome features.

"Is that what you really think about my place?" she asked calmly.

"Of course it is," he snapped. "And so would you if you would come down out of the clouds and face reality. Who the hell wants to live in the sticks? There's nothing to do, for God's sake."

"I find it peaceful," she said quietly as she allowed

him to usher her from the restaurant to the car. "I also like the fact that it belongs to me. That one acre of land and the cabin belongs to me, Shena McLean. Is that so difficult to understand?"

"Big deal," Kip muttered as he started the car and then jammed his foot on the accelerator. "I thought you would get bored with this silly notion after a while. But you're really serious, aren't you?"

"Of course I am. In fact, as of tomorrow I no longer have an apartment in town."

"Have you considered just how damn inconvenient it is having to drive out to the *country* each time we have a date?" he asked sneeringly.

"As a matter of fact I haven't found it particularly inconvenient," Shena said coolly. Nor had any of her other friends, she thought grimly as she sat stiff and erect in the passenger seat and stared straight ahead.

The minute the car came to a stop in front of her cabin, Shena turned to get out. "Aren't you in a bit of a hurry?" Kip asked in that teasing voice that had always been so appealing. He slipped an arm about her shoulders and tried to draw her to him. "It's not like you to pout, Shena love."

"Is that what you think I'm doing?" Shena asked. She shrugged off his arm, suddenly not wanting him to touch her.

"What would you call it?" he went on, an indulgent smile coming to his attractive mouth. "I was critical of your little adventure and now you're paying me back."

58

"You really think that, don't you?" she asked quietly. She dropped back against the seat and thoughtfully regarded him, remembering the many times Win had tried to open her eyes to Kip's selfishness.

"Of course. And I understand. I happen not to like criticism myself. But this—this communing with nature"—he waved a hand toward the cabin—"I honestly don't see why you want to bury yourself in this place."

"It appeals to me exactly the same way your lifestyle pleases you. Frankly, I could never be happy with the constant round of partying that you find so necessary."

"But that's different," Kip said dismissively. "The advertising field is competitive and demanding. When I'm through for the day, I need to unwind. Having a few drinks with friends relaxes me."

"Believe it or not, Kip," she said icily, "owning one's own business and working twelve or fourteen hours a day to keep it going isn't exactly child's play. I also have competition with other nurseries and flower shops. Even the larger grocery chains have their own plant displays. So if I happen to find 'communing with nature' more to my liking than having to deal with a hangover each morning, I'm afraid you'll simply have to accept it."

"Oh I'll accept it for the moment," Kip replied, the confidence in his voice bringing an angry glitter to her eyes. "I'm sure you'll tire of the routine after a few months."

"Don't count on it," Shena told him from over her shoulder as she opened the door and stepped out of the car.

"I'll pick you up at seven tomorrow evening for dinner," Kip informed her, ignoring the frigid look she'd given him. "Why don't you take a change of clothes to the shop in the morning? That way we won't waste time."

"Dinner sounds nice, Kip, but I have other plans." Shena uttered the falsehood without batting an eye. "Perhaps some other time. Good night." Before he could recover from the shock of being turned down, she turned on her heel and walked away. Her deliberate slamming of the front door was reciprocated by a shower of tiny pebbles and sand against the front of the cabin as he roared away.

Shena leaned against the door, her lips pursed in a rueful slant. She had a sneaking suspicion that her relationship with Kip had just fallen into the same category as the cabin next door, a dream gone sour. With the cabin it had been a simple matter of finances. But with Kip, it was a matter of his ego. He was selfish and self-centered. "And I'm beginning to wonder why I've put up with him for as long as I have," Shena said softly into the dimly lit room.

She was still mulling over that same question some time later as she sat on the sandy bank of the creek, her knees drawn up and her arms wrapped about them. The bright light of the moon cast a silvery sheen over the gently moving water as it dipped and cut its way downstream.

A faint sigh escaped Shena as she sought to draw comfort from the place that had become her refuge. Her grandfather had instilled in her a love for the cabin and the small scrap of land that ended at the creek. In times of disappointment, of heartbreak, it had drawn her like a magnet to its peaceful setting. It was her heritage, her legacy, she thought proudly, and she hadn't found a man yet, Kip included, that she would be willing to give it up for.

Suddenly the sound of a low, menacing growl cut through the moonlit stillness like ice-cold steel! Nerve-numbing, gut-wrenching fear sent Shena bounding to her feet. Her intentions were to turn and face the ferocious wild animal about to attack her, but she had forgotten that she was sitting on the steeper section of the creek bank. Suddenly she found herself flying like a guided missile down the incline. As she fought to stop her headlong flight toward the water, she even managed a quick glance over her shoulder, and wished with all her heart that she had remained ignorant of her fate.

The beast was large and snarling, its huge mouth open, the teeth reminding Shena of wide, sharp pieces of steel, rushing eagerly toward her ready to rip her to pieces. She opened her mouth to scream just as her body hit the icy surface of Willow Creek. The last thing she remembered was a sudden sharp pain in her head and a gurgling noise as she sank into the water.

"By God, Fred! I told you to keep that damn dog away from her," Max shouted.

"Well how the hell did I know she would be wandering around? Normal people go to bed at night," Fred replied in an equally scathing voice.

"And just what would you know about normal people, you foul-tempered cuss?" Max continued to rant, then shifted the unconscious Shena in his arms. "Hurry up and open that door, she's freezing to death."

"The door's locked."

"Locked?"

"Tighter than a drum."

"Kick it in!"

"Have you looked at this particular door?" Fred asked in a nasty voice. "Each panel is one half of a small log. Kick it in yourself."

"Might I remind you that I pay you a very nice salary?"

"My 'duties' do not include deliberately breaking my foot."

Max turned first one way and then the other, throwing a harassed glance toward the solidness of the cabin, a stream of curse words pouring from his mouth. "Then break a window. We've got to get her inside."

"I re—"

"Please . . ." Shena murmured. She raised one hand to her throbbing head, wondering why on earth everyone was shouting curse words and why she felt as though she were being spun round and round? And just who was it that wanted to kick in her door?

"Shena?" Max's voice shook with relief as he abruptly halted his tirade and the swinging motion that was making her seasick. "Shena?" he repeated, quickly sitting on the edge of the porch and easing her head into the crook of his arm. "Thank God, you're all right."

"Of course I'm all right, you big, ugly brute!" she exploded, then immediately regretted having raised her voice. Her head felt as though thousands of teeny tiny men were hammering on her scalp.

"Ahh, our Miss McLean is making a rapid recovery, Fred," Max remarked dryly. "She seems to have regained her sparkling wit and charming manners."

"How did you happen to be at the creek?" Shena asked. Opening her eyes even to mere slits was causing her head to swim crazily. "Did you see that awful wild animal that almost attacked me?"

"Fred saw the whole thing and yelled for me. As for the 'wild animal,' I'm afraid it was my dog that frightened you."

"Your dog?" She opened her eyes then and immediately clutched her head with her hands. "Ohhh," she whispered, her face contorted with pain. Not only had she been frightened out of her mind, she thought dazedly, she must have hit her head on a log.

"What's wrong?" Max's deep voice boomed in her ear as he lurched to his feet, his eyes wild with concern. "Dammit, Fred, I told you we should get her to the hospital. Quick, go get the car."

"No . . . please," Shena said weakly, reaching out with one hand and grasping a hard, muscled upper arm. "Please, if you'll only stop swinging me around and put me down, I'm sure I'll be all right."

"Do you want me to get the car, Max?" Fred asked.

Shena cracked open one eye as she was lowered to the ground and glared, as well as she could manage, at the stiff-necked Fred. "No, Max damn well doesn't want you to get the car, you rude, overbearing twit! I have a mind and can think for myself and I also have a mouth to speak for myself." She had every intention of turning and stalking into the cabin, but the arm at her waist refused to budge, and the warm body that was still holding most of her weight inched even closer.

"But Max pays my salary, miss, you don't," the "twit" calmly reminded Shena. He further surprised her by the show of a flickering grimace she thought could possibly be a smile. "I feel responsible for what happened to you, considering I was the one taking Nathaniel out for his nightly walk."

"Nathaniel," Shena repeated. "Who or what is Nathaniel?"

She felt Max turn his head, then heard the one-word command: "Come." From out of the shadows Shena saw a large sable and black German shepherd coming toward them, his head carried proudly, his ears erect.

At the command to sit, the dog obeyed without the slightest hesitation, then cocked his massive head to one side, his intelligent gaze curiously regarding the wet, shivering Shena.

"Ohhh," she softly cried, "he's beautiful. But"—an expression of bewilderment clouded her face as she stared at the now docile animal—"a few minutes ago he was ready to tear my head off. Why?"

"He was merely doing what he is trained for," Max told her. "Nathaniel is a guard dog."

"When did you get him?" she asked, amazed. And why did he need a guard dog?

"I've owned him since he was a pup." Max grinned. He reached out with his free hand and scratched the dog on the head. "He's been staying with a friend of mine in New York. I had him flown down this morning."

"How . . . nice," Shena murmured faintly, wondering what other little surprises awaited her in the days ahead. At the moment she had a neighbor she knew nothing about, who employed a man to do God knows what, and now they were calmly introducing her to their guard dog!

CHAPTER FOUR

"I trust you did think to take your key when you went out?" Max asked.

"Of course." Shena forced a hand into the wet pocket of her slacks, her fingers closing around the cold bit of metal. "Here it is."

Max took the key, then tossed it to Fred, ordering him to open the door. Max then picked up a protesting Shena and carried her inside.

"I'm not an invalid, you know," she remarked spiritedly as he set her on her feet. Being carried around by a giant left her feeling out of control of the situation, not to mention the ridiculous sensation of giddiness that swept over her when she was in his arms.

"I'm sure you aren't. But a blow to the head, such as you obviously suffered, can't be taken lightly." There was concern written all over Max's face, and for a moment Shena decided that perhaps he wasn't so ugly after all.

"Why don't I put on a pot of coffee?" Fred, a silent witness to the exchange of words between his boss and their new neighbor, suggested. "With your permission, of course." He inclined his gray head toward Shena.

"Coffee sounds great," she hastily replied. "You'll find everything in the kitchen." There was a look of chagrin on her face as she recalled how rudely she'd snapped at him earlier. The poor man had simply been doing as instructed by Max. But she got the idea that an apology wouldn't be appreciated by Fred. "If you will excuse me, I think I'll scoot and change into something dry."

"I'd like a good stiff shot of whiskey a hell of a lot more than coffee." Max scowled as he followed Fred to the kitchen. "That was too close. She could have drowned."

"But she didn't, so stop charging about the room like a bear with a burr in your behind," the ever-caustic Fred scolded. "Concern yourself with what will happen if Miss McLean has a 'habit' of taking midnight strolls. It could get rather sticky, don't you think?"

Max swung around and glared. "You're just full of brilliant ideas tonight, aren't you? I seriously doubt one tiny female, no bigger than my fist, is likely to screw up our plans."

"I'm sure Mata Hari was viewed in the same light as she calmly went about her nefarious spying expedition," Fred snorted as he measured coffee and water into the coffee maker. "Why is it that a sane, intelligent man can turn into a blithering idiot when he's faced with a pretty face?"

"Are you suggesting that we get rid of a certain pretty face?" Max threw the question at him.

"I'm suggesting, as I have from the beginning, that this is one of the most insane ideas you've yet to come up with. This time, the risks are too great," Fred threw over his shoulder.

"Well that certainly isn't Miss McLean's fault," Max remarked acidly. "Although I will admit I'd feel a whole lot better if she weren't living next door."

"My sentiments exactly," Fred muttered.

"But I doubt the reasons behind our sentiments are the same," his boss was quick to point out. "You hate women. Having one within fifty miles of you causes you to break out with hives."

"They are a treacherous lot." Fred defended his stand. "A person would find more loyalty in a snake."

"Ahh." Max grinned maliciously. "But a woman has so many more charming attributes than a snake, don't you think? Look at our neighbor, for example. She's pretty, independent and quite a nice little armful."

"She's also mean-tempered, foul-mouthed and is something of a shrew."

"Well then, the two of you should get along famously, shouldn't you? Living with you is like being housed with a flinty-eyed harridan."

"I'm sorry for being so long," a breathless Shena told the men as she hurried into the room, saving Fred from having to respond. She was swathed in a

68

thick blue terry-cloth robe. Her still-damp hair was wrapped in a towel.

"How is your head?" Max turned and stared at her, his alert gaze slipping over her slim body to the scrubbed freshness of her face without a speck of makeup. "Is there any pain?"

"The pain is almost gone, and I feel much better," she assured him. She sniffed appreciatively and smiled at Fred. "That coffee smells delicious."

"Fred only makes delicious coffee," Max told her sourly as he stepped forward and pulled out a chair for her. "In fact, everything he does is perfect. If you don't believe me, just ask him."

Shena looked uneasily at each man, wondering if this was the way they normally carried on or if there was some particular reason for the tension zinging between them. "I'm sure Mr. —" She paused, a frown creasing her brow as she stared helplessly at Fred. "It's just occurred to me that I haven't the slightest idea what your last name is."

"Lister," Fred supplied.

Fred filled three mugs with steaming coffee and brought them over to the table. He very correctly served Shena first, unceremoniously plunked Max's mug before him, then drew out a chair and sat down.

Shena raised the mug to her lips, her eyes brimming with amusement as she watched the two scowling men. She distinctly remembered Fred reminding her that Max paid his salary. Theirs had to be one of the strangest employer-employee relationships she'd ever encountered. "You never did tell me what made you choose Jacksonville as a vacation haunt," Shena began. Perhaps it was time she tried asking some questions of her own.

"Health reasons," was Max's reply.

"Weather," came Fred's simultaneous response.

With a resigned sigh, Shena favored each of her guests with a suspicious glance. "If I were you, I'd decide on only one reason. It gives the impression that you're hiding something with such vague and diverse reasons for visiting our fair city."

At that precise moment her cryptic words of advice were interrupted by an abrupt sneeze, another . . . and yet another. She reached into the pocket of her robe for a tissue and blew her nose, her eyes watery. "Excuse me," she murmured. "I seem to be getting a cold."

"Do you have any whiskey in the house?" Fred asked, ignoring the fact that Max was glaring at him and that they had been nicely caught in a bald-faced lie!

"In the cupboard next to the fridge," Shena told him.

"Lemons?"

"No, but I have a bottle of lemon concentrate. Why?" she asked curiously.

"Because you are about to be introduced to one of the many god-awful home remedies Fred uses to treat unsuspecting people." Max frowned evilly. "He labors under the perverse notion that in order to be

70

cured, one must suffer. Hence the damn witches' brews he is constantly trying to force down people's throats."

Shena looked at Fred, who had walked over to the counter and was busy mixing something in a glass. "I usually don't take too much medicine," she began, her eyes following the concoction as it was set before her. "I really do appreciate your concern, but I honestly don't think I need this." She started to smile at Fred, only to have the smile end in another sneeze.

"Drink it, Miss McLean," Fred instructed her. "Don't be put off by what Max said. It's only whiskey, water and lemon. He's taken it himself, many times, and profited from it, I might add."

Shena had the distinct impression that if she didn't drink the mixture, Fred would promptly hold her nose and pour it down her throat. She reached for the glass and raised it to her lips. When the last drop was sliding over her tongue, she slammed the glass onto the table, her face turning a dull red.

"If I'm found dead in the morning," she gasped, "it will be your fault!"

"I promise that in a few minutes you will begin to feel one hundred percent better," her unsolicited benefactor informed her.

And it was true. In minutes Shena did begin to feel the effects of the bourbon as it inched its way into each and every part of her body. A slow, consuming glow began to slip over her, and she felt deliciously warm and more than a little tired. How easy it would be to just sink back in her chair and fall asleep. . . .

All at once, Shena sat ramrod straight in her chair. "If you will excuse me, gentlemen, I shall retire." She pushed back her chair and rose swayingly to her feet.

Quick as a flash, Max was at her side, one arm around her waist. "Perhaps I'd better help you," he suggested.

"Indeed not," she archly informed him. "I'm perfectly capable of tucking myself into bed. And I am definitely not issuing you an invitation to join me." Holding her head high, she weaved her way to her bedroom and crawled into bed, blissfully unaware that Max had followed and was watching from the doorway.

"Miss McLean strikes me as being a very unusual female," Fred announced from the sink, where he was straightening up when Max returned to the kitchen a few moments later.

"Oh? In what way?"

"Her determination to make a home out of this cabin, and her struggle to keep her small business afloat. It's refreshing to see a woman taking on the responsibility of running her life without constantly crying on a man's shoulder."

Max regarded his companion with a smirk. "Some men—normal men—like for a woman to occasionally cry on their shoulder. It's supposed to do great things for our egos."

"Then that only goes to show how stupid 'some

72

normal men' are." Fred shot him a nasty look. "Speaking of which, clean off the table while I finish tidying up over here."

"Do I look like a maid?"

Fred turned and let his icy gaze slowly travel over the dingy canvas shoes Max was wearing, and on upward over the faded grayish-blue denims with a number of snags and rents in the fabric, to the equally tattered blue shirt that appeared so thin and threadbare across the shoulders. "What you *are* and what crazy roles you choose to play are poles apart. In the meantime, since you look like a bum, you might as well do something useful."

"One of these fine days you're going to find yourself unemployed, Fred. How does that grab you?" Max challenged. He hooked a finger through the handles of the mugs and dumped them into the sink.

"One can always hope," Fred spoke dismissively. "Have you made certain all the windows are secured? Is that door over there locked?"

"Yes, you old mother hen, I've done my sentry duty." Max gave him a wily grin. "Your baby chick is locked in safe and sound. Would you like me to bring over a cot for you so that you can camp on her front porch?"

Shena awoke from her night's sleep feeling as refreshed as a baby. She looked at the clock beside her bed and was surprised to see that it was only six o'clock, still thirty minutes before the alarm was set

73

to go off. Fred must have put enough bourbon in that drink to knock a mule on its behind, she mused as she snuggled deeper into the covers in hopes of getting a few minutes more sleep. Any chances of her catching a cold from her dunking in Willow Creek had been nipped in the bud by the bitter-tasting concoction.

After several minutes of tossing and turning, she finally decided to get up. She had a busy day at the shop, and getting to work a little early wouldn't hurt.

The events of the evening before danced through her mind as she made her bed, showered and dressed. She was still bothered that she hadn't been able to find out why Max Cramer had suddenly appeared in her midst, moving into the cabin next door. She wondered if he was some wealthy eccentric, with too much time and money on his hands? Yet, the thought of him running from anything, even the pressures of a hectic career, didn't fit. Perhaps he was an actor, exhausted by the rigorous schedule of his profession. But she was positive she had never seen or heard his name before. And with his face it would have been difficult not to remember him. That left only one recourse, she decided. The next time she had an opportunity to talk with her mysterious neighbor, she would simply ask the questions that were buzzing around in her mind. She disliked people who pried. But, she grinned, hadn't he taken their relationship beyond that of two polite strangers by taking her in his arms and kissing her? Hadn't his dog attacked—well, almost attacked—her? Surely either of the two situations gave her the right to ask one or two personal questions.

She was still worrying with the problem when there was a loud pounding on her back door.

When she opened the door she found Max balancing a plate covered with foil in one hand and a thermos in the other. He gave her a sweeping bow from the waist, and in his best adenoidal twang announced, "Your breakfast, madam."

Shena was unable to stop the thrill of excitement racing through her at the sight of him. He was fresh and rested, and big as a wall, and his appearance made the beginning of her day all the better. She recovered her poise and reached for the plate, which had tilted to a precarious angle, and stepped back so that he could enter the kitchen. "This is wonderful," she told him, "but just what have I done to deserve such a treat?"

"Fred has somehow gotten it into his stubborn head that you seem to be in need of attention." Max passed on this information with a perfectly straight face.

Shena looked suspiciously at the plate she was holding and the thermos now sitting on the table. "This isn't another of his home remedies, is it?"

"Oh no. Under that foil is a stack of delicious pancakes and sausage. The thermos contains only coffee. But," he told her with a devilish grin, "I was instructed to make sure you were 'in the pink' before I came back. I was also told to see that you ate every morsel on your plate."

"And if I hadn't been in the pink?" Shena couldn't help but ask. "What then?"

"Then, my dear Miss McLean, you would have begun phase two of the mighty Fred's treatment. No doubt, if you had been found with a cold, he would have set to making one of his foul-smelling poultices, which he would have ordered you to keep in place on your chest until the cold broke or until your hair fell out in hunks from the terrible odor. Whichever happened to come first."

"Thank God for the lemon and whiskey." She shuddered as she turned and set the plate on the table. "Have you ever been forced to endure phase two of his treatment?" she asked curiously as she sat down and motioned for Max to join her.

"Once. I had a hangover that would have killed an elephant. I'd managed to go to sleep, when I was awakened by the foulest odor I'd ever smelled. I couldn't understand what had crawled into my bedroom and died, until I happened to run a hand over my chest and found myself trussed up like a Thanksgiving turkey and stinking to high heaven."

"Thanks for the warning," Shena chuckled. She lifted the cover from the plate and closed her eyes with anticipation. "Mmmm, this smells delicious. Will you join me?" she asked out of politeness, fervently hoping he wouldn't. She was ravenous and planned to eat every bite herself.

76

"No thanks." Max grinned at her. "I've already eaten."

"I got the distinct impression last night that you and Fred were a tad out of sync as to why you came to Florida. Did my question pose a problem?"

"Fishing again, Shena?" Max chuckled. He rested one forearm on the edge of the table, then linked the fingers of his hands as he studied her. He liked the sparkle in her blue eyes, the way her auburn hair brushed against her cheek when she moved her head and the way the tip of her tongue was licking the taste of syrup from her lips. In fact, he found himself thinking, he liked just about everything there was about Shena McLean.

"Do you want the truth?" she asked.

"Certainly."

"Well, I'm positively beside myself with curiosity."

"Fred will be sorely disappointed when he learns that you're a nosy little broad."

"Speaking of Fred"—Shena frowned—"just what is his position?"

"He works for me—I think." Max gave a rueful shrug. "He's also my friend." He glanced at the heavy gold watch on his tanned wrist. "I'm expecting a phone call in a few minutes." He rose to his feet, moving uncomfortably close to Shena. His gaze rested on her slightly parted lips as she looked up at him.

Before Shena had any idea what was happening, Max bent down and touched his lips to hers, the tip of

77

his tongue tasting away the sweetness of syrup from her mouth. "How could that man you went out with last night have been stupid enough not to have stayed the night?" he asked huskily.

"Because he wasn't asked," Shena murmured. Her heart was pumping ninety miles a minute and she was positive he could hear the ungodly clamor inside her chest.

"That's good," Max murmured. "I'm afraid I wouldn't have allowed him to share your pancakes." When his mouth descended upon hers the second time, she yielded to him, unable to control the desire that had overcome her.

It was a rapidly breathing Max who finally withdrew, his tawny eyes glistening with longing for this red-haired, blue-eyed vixen. He framed her face with his large hands, his thumbs softly stroking the lips he'd just kissed. "You just may become a problem to me, Shena McLean, a very large problem."

"There's a call for you, Shena." Chloe's voice floated out over the shade-clothed area where most of the plants and shrubs were located.

"Please excuse me for a moment." Shena smiled at the elderly matron who was torn between two different colors of petunias for a window box.

Making her way to the office, Shena sank into the creaky old chair behind the wooden desk. "Hello?"

"Hi, toots," Win's voice sounded bright and cheerful. "How's business?"

"Hot," Shena replied. She leaned back and propped her feet on the corner of the desk. "What's on your mind?"

"Well, I've been doing some snooping around on your neighbor."

"And?" Her heart leaped into her throat. "What have you found out?"

"Not much, I'm afraid. He opened a checking account here at the bank with a cashier's check drawn on a bank in San Francisco."

"How large an account?"

"In the fiftyish range."

"Do you mean thousands?" Shena frowned.

"I do. So whatever your Mr. Cramer is or isn't, he's not broke. It's certainly not the largest account, but it will keep him flush for a few months. By the way, I might be able to come out when I get done here and do some work on the deck. Do you have plans?"

"No," Shena told him. "As far as I know, I'll be there."

"I thought maybe you would be seeing Kip. I ran into him at lunch. Did you know he's back?"

"We had dinner together last night."

"I'm sure that gave you a new lease on life," he remarked acidly.

"You'll be delighted to hear that we quarreled almost the entire time we were together."

"Whatever it was about, I'm on your side. Oops, sorry, Shena, but duty calls." The receiver was plunked down and the dial tone began buzzing in Shena's ear.

There was a thoughtful expression on her face as she continued sitting at the desk. Max had a fairly healthy bank balance, he paid Fred a salary, not to mention having expensive taste in cars. All of this appeared to be accomplished without any visible means of support. How was he able to arrange that? she wondered. And how was it possible for her to respond to a man she barely knew? How could she feel so comfortable with him and, at the same time, suspect every move he made?

These questions came to mind often for Shena over the next two or three days. She knew the main reason for her thoughts of Max was the inexplicable attraction she felt for him. It was an attraction far removed from her feelings for Kip, something she could neither identify nor ignore. She'd lectured herself for not pulling back and keeping a tight rein on the emotions he stirred in her, lectures that worked beautifully until the object of their dire warnings came into view. He was different in every respect from the men in her life. Other men came and went without causing the slightest ripple. Even Kip did not cause such agitation. And since Shena had met Max, Kip had barely registered in her thoughts at all.

CHAPTER FIVE

Shena tilted her head to one side as a faint scratching sound broke the silence of the early evening. She was sitting at the round oak table in the kitchen of the cabin, wrestling with the problem of the amount of money it would take to pay her bills and the much smaller amount of available cash in her checking account.

When the sound came again, at the front door, Shena pushed back the small calculator she was using and stood, her lips pursed with annoyance.

She wasn't in the mood for company, she thought irritably as she stalked through the living room toward the door. She grasped the doorknob, ready to deal with the unwanted visitor. But instead of finding Win or Kip or some other of her friends waiting at the door, she found Nathaniel.

Shena's mood swiftly changed as she stared down into the big brown eyes quietly regarding her. She knelt down, one hand gently rubbing the shepherd's head. "What's wrong, Nathaniel? Are you lonesome? Would you like to come in and keep me company?"

81

A gentle whimper sounded from the dog and Shena chuckled. "All right." She grinned. "You may come in and guard me."

Nathaniel brushed by her as if understanding every word she'd said, and proceeded to go from room to room, his ears alert as he satisfied himself that there was no one else in the house. Shena went back to her seat at the table, highly amused by the air of authority with which the dog did his duty. Then Nathaniel took a position underneath the table and rested his warm muzzle on her feet.

As she settled back into the more pressing problem of paying bills, Shena found the presence of the large dog to be very comforting. He'd been well trained, she thought as she began writing checks. There was none of the usual excited running back and forth associated with some dogs. He exuded the same sense of calm assurance that was such a vital part of his master's personality.

The moments slipped by and darkness gradually settled over the tiny meadow dotted with tall trees and the slow, meandering waters of Willow Creek. The only intrusions were the two rustic cabins that were nestled against the landscape. When the bright flash of a car's twin headlights suddenly swept the area, it was as though an alien being had entered the tiny paradise.

Nathaniel heard the sound of the car long before Shena. He quickly rose to his feet and went to the door, his ears erect, his large head cocked at an angle as he stood and listened.

Shena watched curiously when, after satisfying himself that all was well, the dog returned to his former position beneath the table. He'd barely had time to get comfortable when there was a knock at the back door.

Again Nathaniel shot to his feet and rushed forward. Shena followed and opened the door.

"Hasn't it occurred to you by now that you are living in the country and should exercise a degree of caution before throwing open your door?" Max demanded in a curt, abrasive tone that immediately had her ready to box his ears for his impertinence.

"I assume you have come for your dog?" she asked just as curtly, pointedly ignoring the wisdom of his remarks.

"No," Max remarked flatly as he brushed by her and walked on into the room. "You seem to be in greater need of Nathaniel's protection than I am." He pulled out a chair and dropped into it. Turning to glare at him, a highly annoyed Shena suddenly noticed the fatigue etched in the harsh lines of his face.

Perspiration beaded his upper lip and broad forehead, and his face was drawn. Slowly the anger building in Shena subsided as she studied the weary slump of his body.

"Would you like a drink?" she asked after careful deliberation. She found it difficult to fight when the enemy looked as though he needed a long nap.

"Please."

As she got out the bourbon, ice and a glass, Shena found her mind a veritable beehive of activity as she tried to imagine exactly what it was that had left Max so tired and in such a fractious mood.

She placed the drink on the table before him, then sat down and began adding stamps to each of the envelopes holding checks she'd written.

"You've been busy," Max finally said after downing almost all of the drink she'd fixed him.

"Bills," Shena said quietly. "And you? What have you been doing?" She looked directly at him as she posed the question and saw the tiny glimmer of amusement in his eyes.

"Sight-seeing." He grinned. He finished off the drink, then held the glass up and looked inquiringly at Shena. "May I?"

"Be my guest," she sighed. She reached for her mug and took a sip of coffee, staring thoughtfully at him as he moved over to the counter. He added another ice cube, a mere suggestion of water and a healthy splash of bourbon to his glass. "You've never told me exactly what is you do, Max. Have you taken a leave of absence from your job?"

He turned from the counter and walked back to the table, his long, easy stride covering the distance in two steps. "I dabble in the stock market," he said without hesitation as he sat back down. "At the moment I suppose you could say I'm unemployed. Does it shock you to learn that I'm not gainfully employed?" he asked mockingly.

Shena shrugged. "I suppose not. Although personally, I don't think I could live that way."

"But think of it," he spoke lightly. He reached for one of the bills spread out on the table and scanned the information and the amount due. "No more of these. Can you honestly say you wouldn't like a year away from the responsibilities you've undertaken?"

"Put like that, I suppose it would be nice," Shena admitted. "On the other hand, I spent a year bumming around Europe with some friends after graduation. I gave a lot of thought to what I wanted to do, so I'm really not anxious to throw it all away."

"Is that your grandfather speaking or you?" Max asked. He propped one elbow on the table and rested his chin on his fist, his eyes moving steadily over her hair, her face and the gentle thrust of her small breasts. Shena felt her cheeks grow warm, and she looked away to avoid his gaze.

"It's difficult to separate the two," Shena replied, and was surprised by her answer. But it was so. Her love for her grandfather, and his for her, had been so deep, so strong, that in spite of the difference in their ages they unconsciously thought alike. "He was wise enough to urge me to go, to see—to be sure of the goals I'd set."

"He sounds like an intelligent man," Max said gently. "I would like to have known him." He looked toward the door and then back to Shena. "Let's go for a walk."

"But aren't you tired from all the sight-seeing you've done?" she asked innocently. He was lying through his teeth and she knew it. Yet, in his smooth way, he'd managed to steer the conversation away from whatever it was he was involved in.

Max rose in one lithe move, then caught her hand in his and pulled her to her feet. "I think I can manage a few doddering steps in the moonlight with a sweet young thing. But what about you?" His mouth curved wryly. "Aren't you afraid that if you come with me, I'll turn into the monster you think I am, do God knows what to you and then toss your poor broken body into Willow Creek?"

Shena gave him a thoroughly annoyed look. "Are you trying to frighten me?"

"Am I succeeding?" he chuckled as he pushed her ahead of him toward the door, Nathaniel following close behind.

"No. I was rather ghoulish as a child and thrived on ghost stories."

"But you have decided that I'm up to no good, haven't you?" The moonlight caught the gleam of his white teeth as he smiled down at her.

"I've . . . given the matter an occasional thought," she admitted grudgingly.

"Only a thought?" he teased. He released her hand, only to drop his arm over her shoulders. Shena felt her muscles tighten momentarily at the feel of his warm skin against the back of her neck. The touch of his arm made her tingle, and she looked up at him anxiously.

"Okay," she said flatly. "I can't decide if you're a bank robber, an escaped convict hiding from the authorities or some wild eccentric involved in a nefarious plot to overthrow the government. Are you satisfied?"

"Of course," he retorted smoothly. "A man always appreciates honesty in the woman he's interested in."

"Why are you interested in me?" she demanded bluntly, regretting the words the moment they fell from her lips. She sounded as though she was searching for compliments.

"Because you're beautiful, you're intelligent—most of the time—and I think an affair with you would be the highlight of my—er—sabbatical."

Shena's first thought was to edge him a little closer to the spot where she'd made her swan dive into the creek and push him into the same deep, black hole. But the odds of accomplishing such a feat were poor and she searched her mind for some other equally humiliating form of punishment.

"Is that what this little trek in the moonlight is all about?" She eyed him narrowly, praying he would trip over an exposed root and do major damage to himself. "Are you supposed to bedazzle me with flowery speeches until I swoon in your arms?"

"I doubt it," Max replied unhesitatingly. "Somehow I don't see you as the type to appreciate flowery speeches and you definitely are not the type to swoon. No, you'll require special handling."

"How thoughtful," Shena remarked stonily. "At least I'm allowed to retain my individuality. That's considerate of you, I must say."

"Oh but I can be much more than just considerate," he told her, his eyes twinkling with suppressed laughter as he glanced down at her. "I can be gentle, generous and quite handy when it comes to odd jobs around your cabin. I'm even a fair carpenter and you already know I'm an excellent mechanic."

"You sound as if you're answering an ad." She frowned. "May I point out that, at the moment, I'm not in the market for a lover. As for your other talents, I'll call you if and when the need arises."

"Is Kip Harris your lover?"

Shena turned her head and stared at him. "How did you know about Kip?"

"Is it some sort of secret?"

"No. But I distinctly remember Kip was out of town when you first arrived. And since there was no opportunity for me to introduce you to him when he came to take me out, how did you know I went out with him?"

"I'm sure I must have heard about it from somebody," Max smoothly replied. "However, you didn't answer my question," he persisted. "Is Harris your lover?"

"Oh dear," Shena began. "You really are in an inquisitive mood this evening, aren't you?" She drew in a deep breath and smiled. "Isn't the moonlight beautiful?"

Max threw a murderous glance at the full beam overhead, not in the least impressed with its glow. "How long have you known him?" he asked tenaciously.

"Most of my life," Shena told him. "Are you planning on staying in Florida for the entire summer, Max?" Two could play this little game, she thought.

"Define 'most' of your life," Max demanded in a biting tone. Suddenly the stroll was anything but pleasant. He'd walked over to Shena's cabin because he'd felt an inexplicable urge to see her, to be with her. She intrigued him with her harum-scarum way of attacking life. And her attempts to wheedle information out of him amused Max. He'd known many women in his life and had enjoyed affairs with a number of them, but none had been like her. He wanted an affair with Shena, but he damn well had no intentions of sharing her with another man.

"He was two grades ahead of me in school," Shena said pleasantly. "Win was only one grade ahead of me. Is there anything else you'd like to know?"

In one swift move, Max brought his other arm in front of her, his hand clasping her waist. He quickly turned her toward him, the glow of the moonlight showing the annoyance in his tawny eyes. "There are several things I want to know, Miss McLean," he confessed broodingly. "But it's fairly obvious that all

I'm likely to get from you tonight are a lot of smart answers. I know a far more enjoyable way to wrap up the evening."

Shena closed her eyes as his mouth swooped toward hers. His lips weren't gentle as they took command. His tongue became demanding, darting and plundering as it searched out the warm sweetness that had become imprinted in his mind and wouldn't go away.

The tiny whimper of response that escaped Shena was caught up by Max and absorbed into the powerful aura of sensuality radiating from him, surrounding her with its staggering force. The strength of his persuasiveness was overwhelming. Shena felt the solid hardness of his body beneath her hands and luxuriated in the feeling.

Suddenly the exciting little tremors his lips were creating throughout her body weren't enough, nor was the searching warmth of his large hands as they ran over her back from shoulder to hip. When she felt his warm hands slip beneath the edge of her T-shirt and run a whispery trail upward to lightly, deliberately, scrape the painful fullness of her breasts, Shena arched against the magnetic force drawing her. She reveled in the contact, moving her body against his hand. Her fingers groped at his shoulders for support, her knees becoming weak from the raging desire that was consuming her.

"Shena . . . ?" The hoarse sound of her name in the ethereal silence brought a tiny frown to her face.

She resented the intrusion, resented the dark nod of caution that had managed to creep into her mind in that brief second. "I want to make love to you, Shena," Max's deep voice sounded muffled against her hair.

And I want you to make love to me, she was crying out in a silent plea. But the sane face of caution that was creeping into the helpless muddle of her thoughts had to be reckoned with. And with the reckoning came a certain fear. Not of Max himself, but of her own staggering realization that for the first time in her life she found herself wanting a man completely. Not the mere companionship of another person of the opposite sex, nor the brief, passing interlude that could occur at the conclusion of an evening. What she was feeling for Max was something she'd never felt in her entire life. She wanted to feel him . . . all of him . . . around her, against her and in her.

"No," she whispered without conviction. The slow withdrawal of her hands from his body brought a harsh sound of disapproval from Max.

His hands cupped the boyish slimness of her buttocks and arched her against his hips, reemphasizing his growing arousal and need for her. "What's happened to that determination, that single-mindedness, that dominates your life?" Max whispered. "Are you afraid to let your emotions go?"

"I honestly don't know." Shena stared up at him, the turmoil within her showing in her eyes. She'd never felt so vulnerable, so close to teetering over the edge. Only moments ago she'd felt happiness rushing through her veins like a rampaging river. Now she was like a person who reached out for the brass ring of life only to find her hand empty when she drew it back again.

"Is it Harris?" Max asked in a voice as flat and cold as the razor edge of a steel blade. And even though she had denied him, he still kept his hands on her hips, kept her pressed hard against him. He had no intentions of making it easy for her, he told himself. If he pushed, he knew he could have Shena. But something held him back, he could not force her. He wanted her to come to him willingly.

"Kip has nothing to do with my decision not to go to bed with you." She was calmer now. She wasn't trembling nearly as badly as she had been moments ago. If he released her, her legs just might hold her up.

"I do mean to have you. You realize that, don't you?" Max told her after a quiet moment of thoughtfully studying her. "Your response was too spontaneous, too beautiful, for me to simply walk away and let it go at that. And even if I wanted to, I'm not sure I could."

"Don't rush me, Max." Shena drew a shuddering breath. She knew she should move away from him, but for the life of her she couldn't do it. Not just yet. "I have my own way of reaching decisions."

He smiled then. "You mean tomorrow you aren't

going to stare holes through me and pretend this never happened?"

"No," she said softly. "I doubt I'll ever forget what happened here tonight. But it doesn't necessarily mean I'll hop into your bed either. I've never been involved in an affair. And from what I've seen of my friends who have, I'm not sure I'd like the arrangement."

Even if she had wanted to run and hide from Max the next day, fate was against her. Soon after the day began Shena was ready to explode—right after she wrapped the VW around Win's neck!

The ugly little car wouldn't start. Shena cursed it, she pleaded with it, she kicked it. But it remained as unresponsive as a rock.

She was on the verge of going inside and calling a taxi when Max drove up. Shena threw him a nasty glare, which he returned. From the looks of it, Shena determined that he was coming *from* the interstate, not from his place, and he looked as though he hadn't been to bed at all.

"Well?" she snapped at him as he sat watching her hop around her latest cross like a mad bantam hen. "Are you going to just sit there or are you going to get off your worthless behind and see if you can get this pile of junk moving?"

"Why, of course, Miss McLean," he drawled mockingly as he opened the door of the Bronco and stepped out. "I'd be happy to accommodate such a charming lady as you. The manner in which you 're-quest' my services nearly takes my breath away."

By then, he was beside her, and Shena got a good whiff of his breath. "Just standing by you takes *my* breath away," she bit out, squinting her eyes against the early morning sun and glaring at him. "What on earth have you been drinking?" His clothes didn't look any better than he smelled either. The shirt he was wearing was creased and rumpled, and his pants bore a long greenish-black smear that looked like axle grease.

"Sight-seeing is a time-consuming business," Max threw over his shoulder as he raised the back lid of the VW and poked his shaggy head beneath.

"Sight-seeing?" Shena hooted derisively. "Do you honestly expect me to believe a story like that? About the only thing I'm fairly certain of is that you haven't been with another woman."

"How, pray tell, have you arrived at that conclusion?" Max came out of his hiding place, an expression of complete innocence on his face.

"Because you stink like a pig and your clothes are filthy," she said bluntly.

"I doubt all the women in this part of the world would let a little thing like that stand in their way," he told her with a lecherous gleam in his eyes. "I'm a fantastic lover, you know."

"I'm sure you are," Shena replied scathingly. "In the meantime, will you please try to figure out what is wrong with that excuse for a car so that I can be on my way?"

"I've got a better idea." He reached into his pants pocket for a key and pressed it into Shena's hand. Then he took her by the arm and led her, protesting every step of the way, to the Bronco. "Stop fussing," his voice was firm. "I'm pretty sure your battery is dead. If that's the case, we can stand here and pray over it all day and not a damn thing will happen."

"But what if I have a wreck?" she wailed, and was momentarily gratified by the bleak look that came into Max's eyes as he remembered her previous exploits behind the wheel.

After bringing that tiny bit of sunshine into his life, Shena thrust the key into the ignition and started the engine. She turned the Bronco around and spun gravel as she took off.

"Wouldn't it be cheaper and less time-consuming to just buy her a new car?" Fred asked as he stepped from behind Shena's cabin and walked over to where Max was standing in a cloud of dust and cursing a blue streak.

"Certainly, Fred," he snapped. "I'll buy the car and let you present it to her. Then I'll take *you* to the hospital and have the buckshot picked out of *your* ass after she shoots you for insulting her."

"Ahem—" The unflappable Fred carefully studied the situation. "Perhaps that wasn't such a good idea after all." He cast a disapproving eye over his employer's state of attire, then sniffed, his long nose quivering distastefully. "Is it necessary to throw yourself so completely into this little game you're playing?"

"Don't you start," Max warned him. "I've already been raked over the coals by Mean-eyed Pete McLean. Things didn't go as I'd planned last night, and I almost got caught."

"Then get out while you still can," a sober-faced Fred advised. "It's not worth risking your life."

"There's too much invested to get out now." He shot the older man a shrewd glance. "We've been in worse situations, so stop worrying."

"Then why don't you go find yourself some female companionship?" Fred asked acidly. "As usual, you become impossible to live with when there's no woman in your life."

"For once I agree with you, Fred," Max murmured thoughtfully. "Unfortunately, the woman I happen to be interested in is as stubborn as a jackass. Does that make you happy?"

"I'm ecstatic." Fred grinned. "Knowing Miss McLean as I do, you should receive an excellent lesson in humility."

CHAPTER SIX

It was one thing for Shena to tell herself that any attraction she might feel for Max was futile. It was quite another thing to make herself believe it. He stayed in her thoughts as persistently as a bloodhound on a trail. His image seemed to be printed in her mind. And though she went about her work in her usual fashion, he was constantly with her.

"Has something happened to the business in the last few days that you haven't told me about?" Chloe asked as Shena walked behind the wooden counter to fetch a paper towel and wipe the perspiration from her face.

"Not that I can think of," Shena told her. "Why?"

"Because you haven't been yourself lately," the practical brunette said bluntly. "Yesterday you failed to point out to Mrs. Reese that now was the worst possible time to dig up her side bed and add new shrubs. I've caught you talking to the weeping fig on two different occasions this morning, and you didn't even notice that Charlie was watering that special order of mums from the top with the mist sprayer. Are you trying to destroy your own business?"

"Seems that way, doesn't it?" Shena sighed disgustedly. "I suppose I've been daydreaming."

"Is the handsome Kip responsible?" Chloe made no attempt to mask her dislike for the man. Shena couldn't help but grin at her friend's rather abrasive manner and her lack of finesse when she was on one of her prying expeditions.

"Hardly. The last time I saw him, we didn't part under the friendliest of terms."

"Well at least that's in your favor."

"I do hate to disturb your peace of mind"—Shena grinned—"but I'm having dinner with Kip this evening."

"Then you should see a psychiatrist."

"You are as terrible as Win." Shena frowned. "Kip isn't as bad as the two of you make him out to be. I'll admit his ego is a little oversized, but once you get beyond that, he can be a nice person." What he is, is spoiled and selfish, an annoying voice whispered in Shena's ear. She'd accepted the date with Kip purely out of curiosity and, she grimly admitted, as a desperate attempt to place some distance between herself and Max.

"If you say so," Chloe replied noncommittally. "If I had an unattached male such as Max Cramer living next door to me, you wouldn't find me even considering another man. I'd be camped on his doorstep.

From what you've told me, it sounds like he gives off excitement like some supercharged engine."

"Oh he's exciting, all right," Shena remarked grimly. "The only trouble is, I can't decide which side of the law he's on."

"You're kidding!" Chloe exclaimed, her eyes rounding comically. "Tell me more."

"That's just it," Shena said flatly. "I don't know any more. Every time I try to find out anything about him, I'm warded off with some ridiculous tale that a two-year-old wouldn't believe."

"Have you had a go at the man that works for him?"

Shena nodded. "He's just as bad. Another thing that puzzles me is that on two separate occasions I've heard a large truck going past my place in the middle of the night. Both times I was awakened from a sound sleep. Yet, when I mentioned the incidents to Max, he pretended not to have heard anything."

"Could the trucks have gone on to one of the other cabins farther down from you?" Chloe asked excitedly.

"Not unless the driver knew some mysterious route through a thick stand of pine trees. If you remember, the road that leads to our places serves only those two cabins."

"Maybe he's a spy," Chloe enthused dreamily.

"He may be," Shena muttered, irritated that Chloe was so in his thrall, "but for which side?"

"You have no sense of adventure," Chloe scoffed.

Just then, however, a customer waved to her from the enclosed area where the interior foliage plants were located, and Chloe reluctantly went to help.

Adventure is the least of my worries, Shena thought ruefully as she went off to find Charlie. Just knowing Max was proving to be an adventure. One with which she hadn't the slightest idea how to cope.

Several minutes later a grumbling Shena was climbing a rickety ladder toward one of the numerous rows of support beams that ran the length of her shade-cloth area. She needed to make some repairs. It was a job she detested, but one that was necessary in order to protect her inventory from the elements.

"Keep it taut," she yelled at Charlie, who was at the other end of the beam holding the cloth firmly. She reached into her pocket for a nail, grasped the hammer and began reattaching the ends of the cloth to the two-by-four frame.

The work was slow and tedious. If the cloth was pulled too tight, it would tear. If it was left too loose, it would bag and dip and the weight of it would soon tear the ends from the nails. The section being repaired had torn loose after a heavy rainstorm and high wind several nights before.

"You'd better move that ladder over, boss," Charlie yelled anxiously as he watched Shena, her arms and body fully extended, reaching for the few remaining inches.

"I can make it . . . I think," she managed to grunt, stretching her arms as far as she could. She inched sideways, her midriff flat along the board and only the tips of her toes resting on the ladder.

Suddenly she felt a grip of steel on her ankles and heard a thunderous voice roar, "What the flaming hell do you think you're doing?" She was nearly toppled from her precarious perch.

Before she had time to throw a murderous glare at the intruder, she found herself being yanked to the ground and swiveled around face-to-face with a steely-eyed Max.

His hands were now affixed to her upper arms and he looked ready to shake the living daylights out of her. "Do you get up each morning and spend time and thought on how best to endanger your life for that particular day?" he shouted at her.

"Don't you dare shout at me," Shena hissed. "And take your hands off me," she ordered him, her cheeks turning a brilliant red as she imagined the show they were putting on for the customers.

"Not until you turn around and take a good look at what you would have landed on when you fell," he lashed out at her.

"If I had fallen, Mr. Cramer." She jumped at the chance to correct him. "If I had fallen."

"If—my ass," Max ground out. He swung her about with one hand, then pointed with the other toward several rows of shrubs, their tall, slender limbs and foliage supported by sturdy redwood stakes at least three feet tall. "Do you have some convenient method in your mind for transforming those stakes into an air mattress?" he asked roughly.

Shena clamped her teeth against her bottom lip, loath to admit that he was right. "I'll admit it looks dangerous," she finally got out. "But only if one isn't careful."

"Do you call using a ladder such as that one"—he nodded to the dilapidated ladder she'd been on—"careful?"

"It hasn't collapsed once," she told him grandly. She reached up and pushed his hand off her arm. "I assume you had some reason for stopping by and brightening my day?"

"I'll get to the reason for my visit later," Max commented dryly, his frowning gaze studying the various pieces of shade cloth that needed shoring up. "You go occupy yourself with something less destructive and I'll take care of this."

"You can't dismiss me with a careless wave of your hand and take over. Have you forgotten that *I* pay the rent and that this is *my* business?" She glared at him indignantly.

"So?" Max turned back to her, his eyes running possessively over her tiny outraged body. "Regardless of who pays the rent, you still need the shade cloth repaired, don't you?"

"Of course," she snapped.

"Well then?"

Shena paused for a moment. "It's very kind of you to offer," she replied begrudgingly.

Max threw her into a further tailspin by reaching out and catching hold of her stubborn chin, forcing her to look at him. "Listen carefully, Shena," he said quietly. "I very seldom do anything out of kindness. We both know why I'm here, and it hasn't a damn thing to do with kindness or my love for flowers. I don't know a weed from a daffodil. Now"—he released her, turning to grin at a gaping Chloe and an amused Charlie—"let's get this little job out of the way before your boss breaks a leg or worse."

Shena included her two employees and Max in her frigid look, then swung around and stalked to the coolness of the office. She slammed the door with such force, two empty clay pots toppled off a shelf and crashed to the floor.

"Damn!" she muttered, staring at the mess her temper had created. But instead of cleaning it up, she walked over to the chair and dropped into it. She leaned her head back against the cracked leather and stared moodily into space.

Why did her reactions to Max always run to the extreme? she asked herself. Why couldn't she simply treat him with the same casual degree of indifference or friendliness she usually accorded most men? But the answer to her disturbing ruminations were equally perplexing. There wasn't another man she knew who could turn her into a woman begging to be loved one minute, then with a few well-chosen words have her ready to commit murder the next. But Max could. He had found her panic button on both sides of the emotional fence.

She also knew that part of her fascination with him was the sense of mystery surrounding him. It intrigued her, and at the same time left her with a sense of unrest. Though she often gave the appearance of being slightly flaky, Shena knew in her heart that she longed for a feeling of security—in her private life as well as materially. She wanted the solid strength and love of a man she could depend on. Max offered none of this, and she was angry with herself for her inability to dismiss him from her mind.

Chloe swept into the tiny office with a dreamy sigh. She let the edge of the door slip from her fingers, then leaned back against it, her eyes closed and a silly smile on her face. "He—is—fantastic!" she enunciated slowly and with feeling.

"Oh?" Shena eyed her nastily. "Is he using the ladder or is he levitating?"

"Don't be childish. He can't exactly be described as handsome, can he?"

"Hardly."

"But can you possibly imagine a man like that making love to you?"

"It doesn't bear thinking about. You know you sound like a nut, don't you?"

"I wonder if he has a friend?"

"Take *him*."

"He wants you. I make it a point never to go after a man who is committed to someone else."

"It's a one-sided commitment, believe me. I'd sooner go to bed with a grouchy tiger."

"I'll remind you of that remark after the event takes place."

"How do you know it hasn't already taken place?"

"Don't be obtuse, Shena. You're seeing that toad Kip this evening, aren't you?"

"You have one minute to vacate this office. Failure to do so will bring a pink slip in your pay envelope."

"After what I saw out there, how on earth can you resist?"

"You have forty seconds . . . thirty-nine."

Chloe turned, laughing, to the door. "I've a feeling Max isn't going to like your going out with another man."

"I'm my own boss," Shena muttered stonily.

"So you are," Chloe chuckled brazenly. "But does that mean you can't have a lover? Think about it," she threw over her shoulder, leaving as dramatically as she'd entered.

Shena took the day's receipts from the cash register and dropped them into the cavernous shoulder bag sitting on one of the stools.

"Aren't you going to make a night deposit?" Max asked. He was leaning against the counter watching her. The shade cloth was now neat and taut, as were several pieces of the heavy plastic that enclosed the walls of the greenhouse.

"I'll get around to it in a day or two," she said

105

without looking at him. He'd deliberately stayed until Chloe and Charlie left, and now they were alone. "You did an excellent job on the shade cloth," she added.

"Thank you, Miss McLean." He tipped his head and smiled. "Do those few words of praise mean you aren't still angry at me?"

"Perhaps I overreacted," she reluctantly agreed. "But I resented being made to look foolish in front of Chloe and Charlie, not to mention my customers."

"Making you look foolish was never my intention," Max said quietly. He stepped closer, neatly boxing her into a corner. "You frightened the hell out of me when I looked up and saw you spread-eagled over those damn stakes."

Shena looked at him and it was her undoing. Her gaze became riveted to his mouth. She was barely conscious of his hands as they slipped into place against the wall on either side of her head. Her entire body was trembling with surge after surge of excitement as she anticipated his touch.

Max leaned slowly toward her, his lips feathering their way across the delicate line of her jaw. His tongue traced the outline of her lips, then slipped between them and met the welcoming tip eager to become embroiled in an erotic game of touch and chase.

"Let's grab a bite to eat, then go for a drive," he murmured between a soft rain of kisses against her face. "I want to be alone with you."

106

"I can't," Shena whispered as she searched breathlessly for the bobbing target of his bottom lip.

"Why not?"

"I have a date."

Her answer brought an abrupt halt to the movements of Max's head. He pulled back and stared down at her, his expression guarded. "Who are you seeing?" he asked in a voice so emotionless Shena felt the hairs on her neck stand on end.

Goodness! she thought, maybe he really is a spy. Anyone who could turn emotion off and on with such abruptness had to be a master of deceit. "I'm going to dinner with Kip."

"Ahh yes, the 'golden boy,' " he drawled silkily. "Are you still nourishing the schoolgirl crush you once had for him?"

"Who told you that I had a crush on Kip?" She frowned. Suddenly she didn't like the corner she was in or the menacing air of calm he was showing.

"I'm sure I must have heard it during one of my sight-seeing stints."

"Perhaps you'll invite me along the next time you go out," Shena suggested. "I'd make an excellent guide."

"I'll think about it. In the meantime, don't get any foolish notions while you're out with Harris."

"Such as?" she asked breathlessly.

"Such as thinking you can rekindle something of the feelings you used to have for him." One large hand found its way to her waist and slowly traced a whispery line that brushed against her breasts, then settled on her slight shoulder. "Those feelings no longer exist, Shena. And another thing, be home early," he warned her.

"I don't punch a time clock when I go out on a date."

"In the future there will be no reason for you to do so," he added smoothly. "After tonight you'll be going out only with me."

"Are you threatening me?" Shena asked with a sparkle of defiance in her flashing blue eyes.

"Oh no," Max quickly assured her. "I think it's only fair that you have a chance to lay your childish fantasies to rest, once and for all."

"How kind. Are you sure you wouldn't like to come along with us? I'm certain that if I explained it to Kip the way you've just done for me, he would be delighted to have your company."

"I'll . . . pass," Max solemnly replied, his lips twitching suspiciously. "I will follow you home, though."

The moment she arrived home, Shena threw herself into detailed preparations for her date with Kip. It was as though there were some unknown force urging her to do everything possible to ensure that the evening be a success.

After giving a disappointed Nathaniel nothing more than a quick pat on the head, she hurried inside the cabin and headed straight for the bedroom.

108

Rather than a quick shower, she took a long, leisurely bath, then shampooed her hair. She even added a half-hour rest with a pillow beneath her feet and a plump slice of cold cucumber over each eye to the beauty routine.

She wanted the evening to be perfect. She wanted Kip to be at his shining best, engaging her in brilliant conversation and making her feel as though every woman in the restaurant would be watching her with envy in her eyes. She wanted to hear him say he understood about the cabin, hear him ask her forgiveness for being so rude the last time they were together. She wanted the assurance that Kip *was* as she'd always insisted to others: warm, thoughtful and caring.

There was a desperate need within her to insulate herself with Kip's love in order to protect her heart against the sweeping upheaval Max was creating in her life. For despite his faults, there was no mystery where Kip was concerned. He was just as Shena and the world saw him. Max was an unknown, his past and future shrouded in a cloud of deliberate subterfuge.

Shena regarded her reflection in the mirror, chewing uncertainly at one corner of her bottom lip as she eyed the abundant cleavage revealed by the plunging vee neckline of her green dress. One hand went determinedly toward a drawer that held several scarves, then pulled back. She wanted to be seductive, didn't she? She wanted to sweep Kip off his pedestal and have him admiring her instead of vice versa, didn't she? Then leave off the scarf, she silently scolded. How on earth could she be a sexy, bewitching goddess if she swathed her potential in a safe layer of chiffon?

Her success at appearing absolutely ravishing for Kip, which was evident in the admiration in his eyes when he picked her up, brought a glow of happiness to Shena. Their conversation during the drive back to town was lively. It was as though the cross words they'd had the last time they were together had never been uttered.

"Have I told you that you look lovely this evening?" Kip murmured in her ear as they were being shown to their table.

"Yes you did." She smiled over her shoulder at him. "When you picked me up and several times in the car on the way. But thank you. Compliments are a girl's best friend."

They delayed ordering dinner, opting for a drink first. When the waiter set the drinks before them, Kip picked up his glass and touched it to Shena's. "To the gorgeous redhead in the sexy green dress." He took a long sip of scotch and water, his gaze lingering on the shadowy hollow between her breasts.

Shena basked in the overflow of his attention, although it did occur to her that Kip's gaze seemed permanently glued to her neckline.

"I'll have to be honest with you, honey. I wasn't sure you'd see me this evening," Kip told her.

110

"Oh?"

He gave her a rakish grin. "I'm afraid I wasn't very nice the last time we were together, was I?"

"No, you weren't," Shena agreed, almost laughing out loud to see how totally taken aback he was by her candor.

"Oh come now," he said in a cajoling tone. "Surely I wasn't that bad."

You were a royal pain, Shena was thinking to herself. But rather than point this out to him, she said instead, "Why don't we forget about that evening? Have you had a busy week?" She knew from experience that there was nothing Kip would rather talk about than himself or his job, and in that order.

"If I do say so myself"—he puffed up like a peacock —"I'd venture to say you're looking at one of the firm's next vice-presidents."

"That's marvelous, Kip," Shena said warmly. "Are you speculating or has something been said to indicate that you will get the promotion?"

Kip smiled. "The boss himself took me aside today and said that when Graves leaves in two weeks I would replace him."

"Then we really have something to celebrate, don't we?"

"Which we will do, as soon as we finish dinner," he told her. "I know you don't care for some of my friends, but there's a party this evening and we've been invited."

"Sounds nice," Shena replied, carefully shielding

her true feelings. "Remember, though, I'm a working girl and I can't stay out too late."

"Nonsense," Kip scoffed. "An occasional late night out won't hurt you." Shena murmured something inconsequential and reached for her drink.

Just as she was swallowing a sip of white wine, Shena caught sight of the hostess leading two men to the table next to where she and Kip were sitting. She looked back at Kip, then did a double take as it dawned on her exactly who the two men were. Why on earth was Win having dinner with Max Cramer? Not only that, but Max was dressed in a perfectly tailored dark gray suit that literally shrieked expensive. The stark whiteness of his shirt and the conservative gray tie lent the perfect touch to his attire. Even his hair had been dealt with and lay smooth and thick against his head.

For a moment Shena wondered if she was seeing Max's twin. Surely this impeccably dressed individual couldn't be the same man she knew, the surly, mysterious brute who lived next door.

112

CHAPTER SEVEN

Shena couldn't believe her eyes.

Kip, seeing the loss of his captive audience, followed her gaze to the next table, a look of displeasure marring his handsome face.

"Shena . . . Kip!" Win called to them pleasantly. "What a nice surprise."

I bet it is, Shena thought sourly, her gaze pinned on Max. He was looking from her to Kip with an air of innocence that made her grit her teeth in frustration.

"Kip, I don't think you've met Max Cramer, have you?" Win asked, ignoring Shena's angry glare.

"No, I haven't." Kip quickly masked his initial annoyance and became Mr. Charm as the introduction was made.

With an air of fatalistic certainty consuming her, Shena saw all her careful planning for the evening ahead go up in the proverbial puff of smoke. How could she possibly throw herself into the role she'd created with Win and Max sitting only a few feet away watching her? She was made even more furious when Win suggested the four of them share the same table, and Kip wholeheartedly fell in with the idea.

With Max on her right, Win on her left and Kip directly across the table from her, there was no longer any doubt in her mind that her neighbor and her "former" friend had deliberately set out to sabotage her date with Kip.

"For a gal who has had a hard day at work, you look remarkably fresh," Max murmured in a low voice beneath the conversation Kip and Win were having.

Shena shot him a venomous look. "Were you hoping to find me looking like a hag?" she snapped.

"Not at all," he calmly replied. His amber-flecked gaze swept over the plunging vee of the dress she was wearing before rising to meet her brittle stare. "Did you have some specific plan of action in mind for this evening?" he asked in a mocking voice.

"I fail to see how my plans for the evening, specific or otherwise, should concern you," Shena icily informed him.

"Oh but they do," Max drawled innocently. "I also distinctly remember telling you not to get any ideas where your friend Kip was concerned." He took another look at her dress and shook his head. "You do enjoy living recklessly, don't you?"

Shena opened her mouth to tell him off but just as quickly closed it. She honestly had no idea what to say in response to his deliberate baiting. And the crowded restaurant was no place to become involved in an argument with the detestable boor anyway. No, she eyed him grimly, she would wait until she was back at the cabin. That way no one could hear her when she told him exactly what she thought of him. She would probably end up her "talk" by shooting him!

Win spent the entire time during dinner refusing to meet the "special" look Shena held in readiness to sizzle him with. Each question she tried to direct to him was expertly parlayed by him into a general discussion. She was barely able to restrain herself from reaching out and choking him. Max, once he'd finished taunting Shena to his satisfaction, spent the remainder of his time subtly questioning Kip.

Shena was irate. She held herself aloof from the conversation, but for all the good it was doing her, she could have excused herself and gone home.

Never had she been so glad to see a meal end. She even managed a cool smile when Max thanked Kip for letting Win and him join them. And then—Kip delivered the *coup de grâce*.

"Why don't you guys come with Shena and me to a party some friends of mine are throwing?"

Shena looked directly at Win. She could almost see the tiny wheels in his mind beginning to spin. With an effort that almost dislocated her knee, she brought the tip of her heel down on the toe of his shoe, her eyes never leaving his face. "Yes, Win," she cooed sweetly, "why don't you and Max join us?" She gave him an extra jab for good measure.

"Er . . . we have an appointment with someone

115

in a few minutes," Win managed in a fairly normal voice. "It is this evening, isn't it?" he looked imploringly at Max.

Max gave every appearance of racking his brain to remember. Finally he frowned, then slowly nodded. "I believe you're right. It is this evening." He included Kip and Shena in a regretful smile. "Perhaps another time."

The party wasn't as bad as some she'd been to with Kip, Shena thought later. Pleading exhaustion from all the dancing, she walked out onto the deck for a breath of fresh air, with Kip's promise to bring her something cool to drink ringing in her ears.

She leaned against the railing and let her gaze wander over the sloping grounds to the side of the house. There was a bitter sense of failure, a resigned acceptance of defeat, weighing heavily in her thoughts. All evening she'd tried to find something in Kip that she could hold on to, something she could use to her advantage in the emotional struggle she was involved in with Max.

Unfortunately, Kip had no more depth than a shallow stream. He was so wrapped up in himself, it was impossible for him to feel, to sense, the needs of others. Now any protection from Max depended on her own cunning, she told herself as she stared into the darkness. She'd tried to wiggle out of facing reality and had failed.

It was a few minutes past midnight when Shena

finally persuaded Kip to take her home and even then he was reluctant to do so. During the drive she deliberately ignored the scowl that had settled over his face. What was the point in arguing about it? she asked herself. She'd known and accepted the fact that he was part of her past the moment Max had walked into the restaurant. Beneath the cloud of anger and annoyance that had shrouded her thoughts during that time, she'd unconsciously compared the two men. What she'd seen hadn't pleased her, but it was there nevertheless.

Kip's kiss at her door left her untouched. After he'd gone, Shena walked through the cabin to her bedroom without turning on any lights. There was an air of restlessness about her as she quickly undressed, exchanging the dress and high heels she'd worn to dinner for a pair of worn warm-up pants and a baggy T-shirt.

After hanging the green dress in the closet, she padded toward the kitchen and out the back door. She wanted to sit on the bank of the creek and stare into the water. Her mind was troubled and she needed the peace and solace of the gently flowing stream to soothe her.

In spite of the turmoil within her, almost as soon as Shena sat down, she felt a oneness with nature. The crush of the party and the ear-splitting noise faded into oblivion as she watched the moon-tipped water slip past her.

Just then a sudden noise caused Shena's head to

swing around in fear. But the sight of Nathaniel loping toward her brought a smile to her face. She waited until the large dog drew level with her and then dropped down beside her. "You're out kind of late, aren't you?" Shena said gently as she buried the fingers of one hand in his thick coat and petted him.

"Not any later than his pretty neighbor," came the sound of Max's voice from the shadows of the trees on her right.

Shena's head swirled around to the other side, an expression of confusion on her face. "But Nathaniel came from that direction," she protested, nodding toward her cabin.

Max stepped out from the protection of the trees and moved toward her. "Actually, he came from behind you. He'd already been all around your cabin and trailed you to the creek."

"And you?" Shena asked crossly, seeing yet another part of her evening ruined by this latest intrusion. "Have you been roaming around as well or were you spying on me?"

"Just . . . keeping a careful check on my property and that of my neighbor," he replied noncommittally. He dropped his large form down uncomfortably close beside her, then leaned back on one elbow and smiled at her.

"Is this something you do regularly or is this evening special?" She eyed him suspiciously. He, too, had changed clothes, and was now dressed in his usual jeans and a loose-fitting shirt.

"Oh it's a habit of long standing, but tonight was definitely special. I wanted to make sure you weren't about to do anything as foolish as letting Harris spend the night," he told her without the slightest hesitation.

Shena let her head come to rest against her drawn-up knees, her eyes skimming along the harsh, almost cruel outline of his features. "You do believe in getting to the heart of a matter by the swiftest route, don't you?" she asked quietly.

"Was I wrong in thinking the idea hadn't occurred to you?"

"I really don't know," she sighed.

"But you did agree to go out with him for all the wrong reasons, didn't you?" he asked gently.

"Wrong from your viewpoint perhaps, but prudent from mine."

"What were your parents like, Shena?" Max asked after a thoughtful pause. "I've heard you speak of your grandfather, but never of your mother and father."

She smiled. "Are you hoping to come up with some dark secret from my childhood that would justify my going out with Kip?"

Max shrugged. "It's been known to happen. You know as well as I do that I scared the hell out of you when I told you I wanted you." He gave her a hard, assessing look. "You also knew I wasn't referring to a 'spiritual' relationship."

"No," she said rather flatly, "somehow I knew that

wasn't what you had in mind. And just to set the record straight, my parents were quite normal. They loved me, each other and my grandfather. They were killed in a plane crash when I was nine years old and I came to live with Gramps. Does that disappoint you?"

"Quite the contrary," Max said, his gaze steady on her face. "Now I know that you were running from me out of fear of becoming more deeply involved."

"And that pleases you?"

"I'm never pleased to see you unhappy," he answered in a voice that sent shivers of excitement down her spine. "On the other hand, I'm conceited enough to feel a certain satisfaction in knowing that you can't sweep me under the rug and forget all about me."

Then, with a steady gesture, he reached out with one hand and pulled her toward him, cushioning her tumble with his body. "I want you closer to me," he told her in a raspy voice. Once he had her situated to his satisfaction, her head on his chest and one of his hands tangled in the curly softness of her hair, he asked, "What decisions have you made regarding Harris?"

"Aren't you going slightly overboard with your questions?" Shena asked without any real resentment in her voice.

"Certainly," he wholeheartedly agreed. "But unless I ask, how else am I going to learn anything from you?"

Shena raised her head, watching him at close range. "I was having a rather nice evening until you and Win decided to join us. Whose brilliant idea was that?"

"Don't you believe in fate?" he asked innocently.

"Not when you're involved." She frowned at him. "And besides, why are you suddenly so chummy with Win?"

"I like him. Is there some reason why we can't be friends?"

"That, Mr. Cramer, is exactly what I'd like to know," Shena bluntly retorted. "You appear in our midst with a tough-looking man who works for you, two new-model cars and a suit that had never been near anything so ordinary as a rack. Add your reluctance to talk about your past, the sneaky way you come and go, plus no visible means of support, and you'll have several good reasons to prevent you and Win from becoming friends."

"Ahh," Max chuckled. "Now I get it. You want to protect Win from me." Her heart skipped a beat as he pushed the hair back from her forehead and pressed his lips to the spot. "Exactly what is it you think I'm guilty of, Shena?"

She gave him a guilty grin. "The last time Chloe and I discussed it I think we had you pegged as a spy."

"For which country?" Max asked solemnly, his eyes brimming with laughter.

Shena reached out and tapped him sharply on the chin. "We haven't decided."

"Why a spy?"

"Why not? You sneak around like one. And you've yet to give me an honest answer to a direct question."

"Does it really matter that much to you what I am?"

"Of co—" Shena became embarrassed by the unwitting confession. On the other hand, she reasoned, why play coy with Max? She certainly wasn't lying in his arms just to observe the heavens! "Yes," she said simply and quietly.

In the next instant Shena found herself with her head pillowed on a muscled forearm, and Max leaning on his elbow staring down at her. His other hand was engaged in the most delightful pastime as it moved with the elegance and grace of a dancer over her body.

"I know you think I'm involved in something shady, sweetheart. And"—he grinned crookedly—"you're partly correct. Unfortunately, I can't tell you about it for several reasons. Not the least of which is your own safety. I will give you my word though that nothing bad is going to happen to me nor will I go to prison."

"Is that magnanimous confession supposed to soothe my ruffled feathers and leave me peaceful and contented?" Shena demanded.

"I like to think it will. I'd also like to believe you could find it in yourself to trust me."

"Sounds worthy and noble," Shena said quietly. "But practical application of those fine words is another matter."

"Is that really the problem or are you afraid because you haven't known me since first grade?" Max asked roughly, his hard gaze boring into her. "You have surrounded yourself with a safe, predictable life-style. Win is your pet puppy on a string. Harris will probably come around in time to the nice, tame slot you have picked out for him. Your business will, eventually, provide you with a comfortable income. Everything in your life has been nice and tidy up until I arrived on the scene."

"Is there a crime against planning my life in a manner that pleases me?" Shena asked defensively. Her life did suit her, darn it. Who did Max Cramer think he was anyway, ridiculing her and her manner of living?

"Not unless something or someone happens along that could bring more excitement and enjoyment into your life than you'd ever dreamed of."

"And you think you're the one to bring about such outstanding changes in my life?"

"I'm positive," he said with such assuredness that Shena smiled. In that moment, Max dipped his head and kissed her. "And so will you be."

Shena thought of willing herself to remain passive in his arms. After all, he was so cocksure of himself, he deserved a certain comeuppance. But her lips blithely ignored the command sent to them by her brain and, after only a moment or two of the delightful featherings and tracings of his tongue against the outline of her mouth, she responded with a fervor that had her sending out faint little noises from the back of her throat. Spy, braggart or whatever, she thought dazedly, his kisses were too potent to be taken lightly.

It was Max who drew back reluctantly, a decided breathlessness mingled with his earlier assuredness. "Still care to argue the point?" he murmured.

The moon cast a rakish glow over the craggy features of his face. But there was also gentleness there, which touched Shena.

"Point conceded," she whispered shyly.

"You know I want to make love to you, don't you?" It was a simple, direct question. Shena realized that. Yet, she was also aware that he wasn't forcing her. What kind of man was it who made his intentions so known, so open, then refrained from adding that extra turn of the screw that could bring about guilt or a sense of desperation from a woman?

"The thought did occur to me."

"So?"

"I need some time to think about it."

"It's not a proposal of marriage, just the simple, beautiful relationship between a man and woman. What's there to think about?" he asked huskily.

"Options," she blurted out without thinking. "I have to consider my options."

Max considered her narrowly, clearly puzzled, but amused. "And when you've worked it all out? Will you send me a message? Perhaps a pigeon—a runner —or even a note attached to Nathaniel's collar?"

"I'm sure I'll be able to come up with something to fit the occasion," Shena informed him firmly. But her thoughts were in a bog. Even a fool couldn't help but know that her going to bed with Max was almost as much a sure thing as the sun coming up in the morning. But in her rule book she made the decisions. Besides, she thought maliciously, deciding to cast one's lot with a "suspect character" deserved more than a mere nod of the head.

She pushed his hand from the taut flatness of her stomach and pulled herself into a sitting position. "I think I'd like to go in now," she said quietly without looking at him.

Max didn't try to stop her, his enigmatic gaze following her until she entered the cabin. For several long moments he continued to stare at the closed door. Then, scowling thoughtfully, he turned back and focused his attention on the rushing stream.

His thoughts turned quickly to the "job" he was presently involved in. Then he thought of his feelings for Shena. It was the first time he'd ever found himself in such a dilemma and it damn sure wasn't a pleasant one. But his involvement in this organization and other similar activities from time to time filled a void in his life.

Unfortunately he hadn't counted on meeting a tiny auburn-haired whirlwind with flashing blue eyes. A soft smile stole over Max's lips, totally at odds with the otherwise harsh features of his face. Shena was unique. She obviously didn't give a hang if he was rich or poor, just as long as he was honorable. That one characteristic alone was enough to please him. Too many times he'd seen that calculating assessment in a woman's eyes. It never failed to set his teeth on edge.

But Shena—ahh, Shena was a woman unto herself. Max knew without a doubt that she wouldn't hesitate to take a swing at him if he provoked her beyond her endurance point and that pleased him. He admired that survival instinct in her that made her a fighter. And just as fervently he loved the warm, passionate side of her that surfaced when she was in his arms.

His business in Jacksonville would soon be over. But somehow this didn't leave Max with the sense of satisfaction it normally did when a job was finished. Unfortunately it wasn't the near completion of the job that was bringing about this unrest, but Shena. He wanted her.

CHAPTER EIGHT

Nathaniel, tiring of the ceaseless pacing of his adopted mistress, flopped down in the doorway of the kitchen. A huge sigh rippled from his large body as he quietly regarded Shena with his soft brown eyes.

The solace she was seeking didn't come to Shena as she puttered about the cabin. She walked aimlessly from room to room, staving off for as long as possible the moment when she would have to come to some decision about Max and her feelings for him.

Her nervous wanderings finally came to a halt in the kitchen. She leaned against the counter and stared out the window toward the lights visible from the other cabin. Max's cabin. In far less time than she'd ever dreamed, he had become a part of her life, a vital and integral part of every day that had passed since meeting him.

She'd become attuned to the sound of his deep, gravelly voice. Her eyes eagerly awaited the sight of him each day. The mystery that surrounded him had become meshed with the doubts regarding his character, leaving Shena sternly disapproving on one hand, while on the other she found herself concerned for his welfare.

Her hand stole to the back of her neck as she sought to bring some order to the hodgepodge arrangement of her emotions and feelings for Max. The wrist against the side of her face still bore the scent of the cologne he used, bringing back the feel of him against her body only a short while ago. She'd wanted him then and, she sighed, she wanted him now.

Shena realized the next move was up to her. Max would never push her, and for that she was grateful. But did she have the courage to tell such a large, intimidating person that she wanted to go to bed with him?

"Why not?" she whispered in the near darkness. She turned and took an eager step forward, then paused, her courage deserting her like a gush of water being suddenly turned off.

Options. She'd told him she had to consider her options. But what options did she really have? Only two. She could share what would inevitably be a brief relationship with perhaps the most exciting man she'd ever met. Or she could bury her feelings for him, let him slip away, and wonder about what "might have been" for the rest of her life.

Shena flinched at the thought. But at the same time, he wasn't being honest with her, she silently argued. It was one thing to become involved with a man who was straightforward about his intentions

128

and his activities. But it was an entirely different matter when faced with a man who made his romantic intentions clear—very clear—but was as close-mouthed about his personal life as a clam.

Ahh, but hadn't he assured her that it wasn't marriage he was offering, but an affair? Did she require a computer printout from a man before she could even begin to contemplate an intimate relationship with him? How could she be such a goose!

A disgusted sigh slipped past trembling lips as Shena considered how cowardly she was. Suddenly she was reminded of something her grandfather had once said during a time in her life when she was torn between two different frames of mind. "Thinking something through doesn't necessarily mean a person will arrive at the most sensible or the wisest conclusion, Shena," he had advised. "There are certain things in life that can only be learned from experience—good or bad." Well, she decided, she definitely didn't want to go through life wondering, now, did she?

Without another thought, Shena turned on her heel and walked to her bedroom. She switched on the lamp beside the bed, then moved over to a chest and opened a drawer. Her small stubborn chin set with determination, she began to inspect each of the three nightgowns she owned.

The first one was a creation in electric orange with a colorful array of daisies scattered down one side of the bodice and around the hem. Shena eyed the garment with the same sinking feeling she'd experienced when she first opened the gaily wrapped package from Win at Christmas. There was no explaining his taste, she sighed as she dropped the gown. She considered the remaining two: a stunning flannel number with long, ruffled sleeves and a high neck, and a blue gown with capped sleeves and a rounded neckline that she knew from past experience made her look about fourteen. Even the material displeased her, she thought, as she rubbed it between thumb and forefinger. It was soft to the touch, but certainly not sheer or sexy.

But what choice did she have? Without further hesitation, Shena took out the blue gown, removed her clothes and slipped the gown over her head.

Once the problem of what to wear was taken care of, Shena stood undecided in the middle of the room, her gaze slowly taking in the antique furniture, the gleaming pine floor with the hand-hooked scatter rugs and the patchwork quilt coverlet on the bed. The setting, while pleasant and peaceful—and one that she'd worked diligently to achieve—definitely wasn't in keeping with the seduction she had in mind. To her way of thinking, such an occasion called for a special atmosphere.

That being the case, she figured, she needed mirrors, mood music, seductive lighting, candles, wine and grapes—it was grapes, wasn't it, that one always saw some sexy siren dropping into a man's mouth? Even if the opportunity didn't present itself for her to perform such a task, she still considered the grapes a necessary prop for the setting she was creating. With those articles of importance whirling in her mind, she began hurrying about, rummaging in boxes and closets as she collected the necessary equipment.

Within the next hour the room underwent a transformation. It was soon far different from the attractive country decor that appealed to the owner. The patchwork quilt had been replaced by lavender silk sheets left over from Shena's first apartment and her fledgling attempt at independence. The lamp on the bedside table sent out a yellow glow, the original bulb having been replaced by a yellow bug light that cast a peculiar sheen on the lavender sheets.

Leaving nothing to chance, Shena had grouped several small candles around a taller, much fatter one. That the larger candle just happened to be of the citronella variety mattered little to her. "At least we won't be bothered with mosquitoes buzzing around," she muttered beneath her breath as she surveyed her handiwork. Besides, she reasoned as she hurried to the kitchen and unearthed the home-made wine Chloe had given her, tall tapers could easily become fire hazards. How could two people, caught up in the throes of lovemaking, keep a watchful eye on spindly candles?

The wine was quickly poured into an attractive decanter. Two stemmed glasses, the decanter and a bunch of plump purple grapes were then placed on a

131

tray and carried to the bedroom and placed on the cedar chest at the foot of the bed. Music, Shena chided herself. How on earth could she have forgotten something as important as music? She zipped around the bed to the table and turned on the radio. Not very romantic, she sighed, but the stereo was on the blink.

As the soft, melodious sounds of strings filled the room, she looked quickly around. Had she forgotten anything? She mentally ticked off each task on her list and, satisfied that she'd covered everything, walked over to the dresser for a quick touch-up of her makeup. When that was done, she automatically reached for her favorite cologne. Her hand stopped in midair. Of course! This softly lit romantic setting should give off a fragrance befitting the occasion, shouldn't it? Without giving further consideration to the number of already strange "fragrances" wafting from the small room, she reached into a dresser drawer and removed a delicately sculptured bottle of perfume—another gift from Win—and removed the tiny gold cap. With a bold move, she walked over to the bed and proceeded to mist the lavender sheets generously with the expensive scent. That left one final move that would set into motion the main event for the evening that was yet to be enjoyed.

With an unsteady hand, Shena reached for a pencil and pad. Before she could change her mind, she wrote a brief, concise message, then tore the single sheet of paper free and went in search of Nathaniel.

The shepherd stood obediently as the note was attached to the leather collar around his neck. Shena straightened, then walked to the back door, the dog keeping a constant vigil beside her. "Go to Max, Nathaniel," she issued the command in a firm voice as she opened the door. As though understanding completely, the big dog darted out into the darkness.

The moment Shena heard the back door open, her hands gripped the magazine she was holding. The tips of her toes dug painfully into the soft oval hooked rug on which she was standing. Oh please! she thought, briefly closing her eyes as she braced herself for the first sight of Max. Please don't let me screw this up, she silently begged. Some of the tension in her small body eased when she heard the sound of a chair banging against the kitchen table, followed by a muffled "Damn!" Shena smiled. That was typical. Hadn't all her encounters with her neighbor been prefaced with a certain explosiveness?

She felt, rather than saw, Max the moment his huge frame paused in the doorway. As though releasing her hold on a lifeline, she allowed the magazine to slip from her fingers. It made a sharp thud as it hit the rug.

Slowly, Shena raised her head and looked at Max. He had obviously just stepped from the shower. His hair was still damp. He'd even taken the time to choose his shirt and pants: light gray shirt and dark gray trousers. He looked powerful and sexy and quite

133

probably the most intimidating person she'd yet to encounter.

Max, during those fleeting moments of Shena's scrutiny, was of two minds. At first glance he was positive someone had whisked away his spirited little fireball and replaced her with a tiny, blue-gowned sprite. She looked about fifteen and as unsure of herself as a kitten in a whirlwind. A strange rush of feeling and warmth swooped over him as he stared at her. It was quite sobering, seeing her like this. He would never be able to erase from his mind the picture of such vulnerability—such innocence—standing before him.

He let his tawny gaze touch on each of the changes that had been made to the bedroom. He had a keen memory, and since the night he'd followed Shena to her bedroom after her dunking in Willow Creek, he well remembered what the room had looked like.

Max's continued silence was causing panic to engulf Shena. She made a slight movement with one hand. "Would you like a glass of wine?" she asked in a subdued voice. This wasn't going right, she thought hysterically. If all the affairs in the world start off this slowly and painfully, how can it be that anyone bothers with them in the first place?

"That would be nice," Max replied as he walked into the room. It felt to Shena as if the room were closing in on her.

"What would be nice?" she asked, her voice quivering with nervousness.

"A drink," he said quietly, and smiled at her. "You offered me one, remember?"

"Oh—yes. So I did." Shena had the grace to blush. She waved him to the one chair in the room. "Would you care to sit down?" Well, she berated herself, they couldn't continue standing in the middle of the damn floor for the rest of the night, could they? How they would get from their present positions to the bed would take a miracle of gigantic proportions!

With jerky movements, Shena moved to the chest at the foot of the bed and poured a drink for each of them from the decanter. When she turned to take Max's to him, she gave a slight start at finding him standing directly behind her instead of in the chair where she had told him to sit. "Must you move about so silently?" she asked querulously.

"Sorry." Max smiled apologetically. He took the drink from her trembling hand, the touch of his fingers against hers warm and vibrant. "Why don't we both sit," he suggested, "on the bed?"

Shena considered the idea only briefly, then did as he suggested. Unfortunately, when the two of them sat down, she found herself slipping like a tiny rock smack against the solidness of his huge body. Before she could correct the situation, Max slid his free arm around her waist, nipping in the bud any ideas she might have had of conducting a polite conversation with several feet separating them.

She had been close to him a number of times, Shena told herself in a frantic effort to calm the erratic clump-clumping of her heart, but those words failed to bring about the serenity she was seeking. There was just simply more of Max to absorb at close range than of any man she'd ever met.

"Shall I propose a toast?" he said, breaking the painful silence.

"To what?" Shena asked suspiciously.

"To us."

"Oh. I—I suppose that would be nice." She dutifully raised her glass to the one he was holding, the soft clink of crystal sounding loud as a drum in her ear.

"To us . . . and to the beginning of a beautiful relationship."

Shena watched with hypnotized concentration as he put the glass to his lips. Her gaze slipped upward over the roughness of his features in time to see the most amazing expression of startlement appear in his face. For one incredible moment it looked as though he were going to choke!

Max lowered the glass and peered into its contents, then stared incredulously at Shena. "Is something wrong?" she asked in a hushed voice. Had Chloe's wine turned to vinegar?

"Er—exactly where did you get this 'wine'?" he asked when he could breathe normally again.

"From Chloe," she told him. "Her uncle makes it. Is there something wrong with it?" she asked worriedly. Darn it! She should have used the bourbon.

"Oh no," Max quickly assured her, his lips twitching as he tried to control his amusement. "Her uncle makes excellent white lightning."

"White—don't be ridiculous," Shena frowned. "This is homemade grape wine." She raised the glass to her lips and took a healthy sip. The second the liquid hit her throat, she felt the breath leave her lungs. She was positive her eyes were permanently crossed and fairly certain each of her teeth had fallen out. A resounding whack on her back by Max brought the world back into focus.

She raised watery blue eyes to meet his twinkling tawny ones. "I've been passing these gifts of wine around to my friends for the last eighteen months," she finally got out in a husky voice. "I've been giving them moonshine, haven't I?"

Max nodded. "The best I've ever tasted," he said unhesitatingly.

"I'll kill Chloe!"

"Don't you dare. Just pass her kind offerings on to me."

"But it's illegal!" Shena exclaimed while visions of being incarcerated floated before her eyes.

"Don't let that little matter bother you," he chuckled at her shocked voice. "If you're ever picked up for bootlegging, I'll hire you the best lawyer in the country to defend you."

"And I'm sure you wouldn't have the least problem finding one, would you?" She eyed him narrowly. "I'm convinced you're only one step ahead of a noose now."

"You may be right," he replied nonchalantly as he plucked the glass from her hand and finished off her drink. She was equally amazed when he did the same with the remainder of the innocent-looking liquid in his own glass. Then, setting both glasses on the tray, he turned to her. "Now that I've been an excellent guest by drinking your 'wine,' why don't we talk?"

Before Shena could reply, she found herself being pulled into his arms as he eased both their bodies to the softness of the mattress. "What do you want to talk about?" she asked in a voice somewhere between a croak and a squeak.

"For starters," Max said gently, "I think the best thing we can do is try to get you to relax."

"I'm re—"

But she never finished the sentence, for her mouth was covered by those same lips she'd watched earlier, as they caressed and coaxed the beginnings of a response from her trembling mouth. With exquisite care, Max turned a simple kiss into an expression of such tenderness and, at the same time, opened the door to a flood of passion so intense that Shena was convinced she would drown from the waves that were crashing against her entire being.

She heard soft moans of pleasure and was surprised to discover they were coming from her. Her body followed the suggestion of Max's hands as they began a sweeping caress over her hips, her stomach and upward to palm the warmth of her sensitive breast through the silky material of the blue gown.

His lips continued their seduction of her mouth even as the capped sleeves of the gown were eased off her shoulders and the bodice pushed down so that she was bare to the waist. The quiet moans turned into short gasps of surprise and pleasure when moist lips dipped down to surround first one small pink nipple and then the other. Her body arched, her hands ran feverishly over the broad shoulders. The maelstrom of feeling buffeting her was unlike any other she'd ever encountered.

Suddenly Max raised his head and looked at Shena, his hands clasping her rib cage tightening as he took a deep breath, then sneezed! The cloud of euphoria surrounding her dissipated somewhat as Shena saw him rest his forehead against her breast, then felt the quick intake of air again and again till he had sneezed at least five times.

"I'm sorry," he finally managed. "This has never happened to me before. I can't imagine what's causing it."

Shena was torn between the insane desire to laugh at the sight of this shaggy-haired giant with his forehead resting against her naked breast as he apologized for the sneezing fit and the urge to box his ears for daring to interrupt what had been the most wonderful experience of her life. Damn his infernal hide, she'd put a lot of thought and effort into this evening. Her "affair" was certainly turning into a strange and bizarre event.

"Perhaps you are allergic to me," she quietly suggested.

Max raised his head and stared, then let his gaze slowly sweep lower till it was pinned on the inviting sight of her breasts. "Then I suppose I'll have to go through life sneezing, won't I?" he replied huskily.

"D-do you think it could be the different fragrances in the room?" she offered hesitantly. His eyes were definitely watering again and even the yellow glow of the bug light failed to hide the red in them.

"Exactly how many are there?" Max calmly asked. "Better still, what are they?"

"Well," Shena sighed, feeling like a ten-carat fool, "there's the perfume I sprayed on the sheets."

Max immediately sniffed the satin material nearest his nose and grimaced. "Er—one of your favorites?" he asked faintly.

"No. It was a gift from Win. He always gives me something wildly expensive that I can't use. Then there is the bug light in the lamp." She frowned. "But that isn't supposed to give off an odor."

"Why the bug light, sweetheart?" Max asked gently, making the question appear as harmless as if it were silly for everyone not to have a bug light in the bedroom lamp.

"I didn't have a blue one," she informed him, then rushed on, "I remember from a sexy book I once read that a blue light does strange and wondrous things to create a romantic atmosphere. I made a mental note to try it someday." She paused. "It must be the candles. The small ones are cinnamon and sandlewood. That shouldn't bother you. Perhaps it's the citronella one."

"Which is that?" Max asked in a strangled voice, the laughter in his throat threatening to choke him.

"The large one in the center." Shena nodded toward the attractive arrangement on the dresser that was casting its glow upon the room. "I thought sturdier candles would be safer than tall tapers. Don't you agree?"

"Indeed," Max murmured, then quickly dropped his head against her breast. At first Shena thought he was about to start sneezing again, but after watching and feeling the shaking of his broad shoulders for a few moments, she realized he was laughing. The toad!

"Move your detestable carcass off me and go home," she demanded in a stern voice. There was no way in the world she would go to bed with a man who laughed at her. Now that she had had time to give the idea more thought, she wasn't at all sure she could go through with this!

CHAPTER NINE

"No." Max uttered the one word as his head shot up and he stared down at her. "You sent me a special invitation, saying you'd considered your options and had decided we should further our relationship. Why have you suddenly changed your mind?"

"No woman in this world enjoys being laughed at," she haughtily informed him—as haughtily as she could manage with his large hands gently palming the sides of her breasts and his thumbs, teasing her nipples, eliciting the most remarkable stirrings in the pit of her stomach.

"I'm laughing with you, sweetheart, never at you," he rasped in his deep voice. "And if you care to compare gripes, I think mine is more embarrassing. I've never been in bed with a beautiful woman only to be overcome with a fit of sneezing and have my eyes water like crazy." He nipped the tip of her nose with his teeth. "That's embarrassing."

In spite of herself, Shena had to grin. "Do you think it would be better if I got rid of the candles and the satin sheets?" she was surprised to hear herself asking. What had happened to her resolve to throw him out of her cabin? she wondered.

Max pushed himself up into a sitting position, then drew her up beside him and pulled her gown back into place. "Sounds terrific. Find me some different sheets and I'll take care of the bed while you douse the candles. Okay?" He grinned.

"Okay." Shena shrugged.

It was amazing, she thought a few minutes later as she carried the candles out onto the deck and blew them out, but being practically naked in Max's arms wasn't the least bit embarrassing. Was it that way with every man? she wondered as she stared into the darkness. Would she feel the same way if it were Kip in her bedroom now instead of Max? She thought of the other men she dated from time to time. Funny, but neither Kip nor any of the others had ever caused her to want to go beyond a good night kiss.

Shena entered the bedroom as Max was tucking the top sheet beneath the mattress. Some of her confidence deserted her when she saw that not only had he removed the satin sheets, but his shirt as well. She stared at the smooth flow of muscles that played in his arms and shoulders as he ran a hand over the sheets. Somehow she had felt a lot safer when he had all his clothes on.

Max, recognizing the beginnings of panic building in Shena, smiled at her, then reached out and turned off the lamp. Perhaps the darkness would help calm her down. He gave a slight shake of his head. Never

143

in his entire life had he encountered such an evening. A sober expression became etched in his features as he watched Shena move hesitantly into the room. He would be willing to bet everything he owned that she was a virgin. And for once in his colorful life, he didn't feel so sure of himself.

"Would you like another glass of wi—er—another drink?" Shena asked across the small space that now separated them.

"Perhaps later," Max replied. He reached out and caught her hand, then pulled her into his arms, the slightness of her frame curving neatly against him. "I have to know something before this goes any further, Shena."

"What?"

"Are you a virgin?"

"Are you?"

"That's beside the point," Max scowled.

"I'm not in the mood for twenty questions, Max," she said after a thoughtful pause. She raised her hands and let her palms gently slide against the dark growth of hair on his chest. "From the moment I decided to ask you over, I've committed one huge blunder after another. At the moment my self-esteem is about an inch high. For some strange reason that even I can't begin to understand, I want to spend the night with you—or what's left of it. If I've been to bed with one, none or twenty men, does it really matter at this point?"

Feeling the hot breath of a familiar threat breathing down his neck, Max asked, "Is it marriage you're after?" It was a blunt question and one he felt like a heel for asking, but some sense of self-preservation was egging him on.

"I really hadn't thought about it," Shena answered honestly. "But I don't think so. I think I like your earlier suggestion best. An affair. I'm at a point in my life where I think it's time to make some changes."

"I see," he said unconvincingly. What the hell was she talking about? Max wondered. Had he misjudged her feelings for that Kip character? Was she using him to get over her feelings for Kip?

"I truly hope you understand, Max, because I'm getting very bored talking." She placed her hands on his shoulders and rose on tiptoe to trace and tease the outline of his lips with the tip of her tongue.

Max sucked in a great gulp of air as a shaft of desire shot through him. Without another word, he scooped her up in his arms and carried her to the bed. His ease and the deftness of his touch made Shena wonder fleetingly how many times he'd performed the task. He removed her gown and the rest of his clothes. The bed gave beneath his greater weight, and Shena soon forgot any concern for what had occurred before this night as a special magic worked its way over her. His hands and lips took control of her body with gentle but determined possessiveness.

His tongue licked its way down over the fragile column of her neck to the pink tips of her breasts, while one hand stroked and cupped the raging fire

145

that had become affixed to the center point of her thighs. With each caress, the desire consuming Shena drew her deeper and deeper into a labyrinth of passion. She could feel her body following the lead of his beckoning, could feel her head thrashing from side to side as she absorbed that first and excruciatingly beautiful coil of need rising and building with intensity within her.

"Don't fight it, Shena love," Max whispered hoarsely against her ear as his lips nuzzled the frantically fluttering pulse in her throat. And she didn't. She couldn't. She was walking a tightrope of joy that threatened, any moment, to collapse and send her into the bottomless pit of longing and need that had awakened in her that first day she'd looked into that pair of tawny eyes.

Suddenly she felt the demanding thrust of his knee between her thighs and the settling of his large body over hers. Strong arms gathered her to him as the gentle rhythm as old as time began. Max guided her through peaks and valleys of ecstasy that left her clinging to him in wonderment. The rapturous journey led them into a fantasy world that alternated between brilliant sunburst and the soothing wonderment of moonlight and, finally, the gentle descent into a valley of such peace and contentment as to leave Shena drugged from the sheer beauty of it all.

When the buzzing sound of the alarm sounded, Shena reached out with one hand to stop its abrasive intrusion. She opened sleepy eyes, her gaze immediately going to the pillow beside her. But instead of seeing Max, there was only the indentation where his head had lain on the pillow.

With a frown, Shena sat up. She drew her knees to her chest, resting her chin on them, her mind taken over with the events of the evening. It had been perfect for her and, she had thought, the same for him. So why had he stolen away in the darkness? she wondered. She'd wanted that first confrontation with him, wanted it in the privacy of her cabin so that she could deal with it in an atmosphere that was familiar. Now Max had taken that opportunity away from her and it didn't suit her at all. It left her feeling uncertain and filled with a sense of dread, wondering at her reaction the next time she saw him—even wondering when she would see him.

Quickly and with more spirit than usual, Shena swung her feet to the floor. Arguing with herself wasn't going to change anything. Max was—Max. She'd been well aware of his unpredictability long before she went to bed with him. And if he failed to fall in with her preconceived ideas of behavior, then that was no one's fault but hers. She still had a business to run, and if she didn't get moving, Charlie would have her bankrupt before noon.

Her flip prediction came back to haunt Shena a couple of hours later as she stood in the middle of a special shipment of white and lavender potted mums. She looked pointedly from the blossoms to the red face of her employee.

"How many times have I told you, Charlie, never to water mums from the top?"

"I'm sorry, boss. Honestly I am," the lanky young man shrugged. "I was pushed for time yesterday afternoon. My schedule is really hectic this summer and I had a test in one of my classes last night."

"Well you'd better hope and pray that not a single speck of brown appears on these mums before they're picked up in the morning. Mrs. Adler wants everything perfect for her daughter's wedding."

"She should." Charlie scowled. "She's lucky to be unloading that pig on some poor fool."

"Charlie!" Shena exclaimed. "That's not a very nice thing to say about a person."

"But that is what you don't understand, Shena," Charlie said patiently. "Marie Adler isn't a warm, kind person. She's a snob. An overweight, bratty snob. If her parents didn't have all that money, she'd never have found a husband, and there'd be no need for you to be standing here lecturing me because a fungus might appear on Marie's mums."

"Well"—Shena struggled to keep a straight face—"just remember in the future. Water the mums from the bottom. Okay?"

"Sure, boss. By the way, our supply of hanging baskets has dwindled down to almost nothing. Do you want me to run out to Mr. Smith's and see what he has? Our sale ad in the paper will come out in tomorrow's morning edition."

"Oh dear." Shena chewed at one corner of her bottom lip. "I'd forgotten. Perhaps—no, you need to stay here and add those broken bags of peat moss to the bare-root bin. And don't forget to use those two bags of potting soil next to the shed. I'll go see what Mr. Smith has for us."

Shena turned to retrace her steps to the front only to find herself barreling into a chest as wide and thick as a tree and just as immovable. Two strong arms reached out and pulled her close.

"Don't you ever slow down?" Max murmured from the top of her head, where his chin was now resting.

"Let me go!" Shena whispered fiercely, her face turning beet red as the grinning Charlie made no effort to hide his amusement.

"Why the hell should I do that?" Max came near to booming, his arms tightening around her as though some unforeseen force was about to swoop down upon them and wrest her from his arms.

"Because, you big lummox," she said icily, wedging her palms against his chest and easing him away so she could look up into his face, "we happen not to be alone."

"We are now," he told her, for Charlie had slipped away. There was a devilish gleam in his brown eyes. "And I want to kiss you."

"Don't!" Shena exclaimed, feeling the touch of his lips against her quivering cheek.

Max frowned. He released his hold on her. "Let's go to your office," he told her in a rough voice.

Keeping her eyes glued to the path directly in front of her, Shena walked purposefully to the small office. Once inside, with the door closed, she started to move behind the desk. But Max wasn't having any of that. He placed both hands on her waist and plucked her off the floor, raising her to eye level.

"Kiss me," he murmured hoarsely.

Obediently, Shena caught his face between her hands and touched her lips to his. From there Max took over. His mouth opened to hers and his tongue thrust boldly between her teeth, teasing and plundering. Had she been standing, Shena wasn't certain her legs could have supported her. She felt her body growing warm and soft in the most delightful places, and felt the hot fiery tip of desire exploding in her.

It was a shaken Max who drew back first, his dark eyes glazed with passion. "I'm sorry I had to leave you this morning," he said, slowly letting the weight of her body slide against the length of him till her feet touched the floor. "I had an appointment I couldn't miss."

"Couldn't you at least have left a note?" She frowned.

"I knew I would see you later in the day."

"But I wanted you to be there when I awakened," she argued.

"Why?" Max asked sharply.

Shena pushed out of his arms and walked the few feet to her desk. "I'm new at this sort of thing." She looked at him over her shoulder. "Since it was the first time I'd been to bed with a man, I wanted our first meeting afterward to be in private, not with other people watching us."

"Why?" Max repeated the word. He crossed his arms over his chest and waited.

"I—wanted any reaction hidden from prying eyes," she said softly. "But now that it has happened, I can see that my worry was for nothing."

"Oh? Does that mean you've already dismissed what occurred between us as unimportant?" he asked in a cold voice that sent shivers down Shena's spine. "Did you suddenly remember something from the past, reminding you not to enjoy life? Perhaps you found yourself wanting to replace me with Kip Harris?"

"How can you say that!" Shena exclaimed. "I enjoyed making love with you more than anything I've ever done in my entire life. It was beautiful. As for Kip, don't you think I could have gone to bed with him long before now if I'd wanted to?"

"Then what's all this about a reaction to seeing me?" Max asked aggressively. He walked over to where she was standing, the closeness of him reaching out to her as potent as if he had touched her.

"I—I wasn't sure how I'd feel," she muttered, nervously shifting a stack of invoices on the desk. "Perhaps I wanted some kind of reassurance from you. Maybe I wanted to see your expression when you opened your eyes and looked at me." She shrugged one shoulder in a gesture of indecision. "Frankly, I don't know what I mean."

"Then let me see if I can help you," Max said quietly. He reached out for her, turning her around to face him, his hands on her shoulders warm and secure. There was tenderness in his gaze as he stared down at her, tenderness and the presence of another emotion Shena couldn't quite identify. "I'm thirty-nine years old, honey. That's quite a bit of difference in our ages by anybody's count. I'm also a hell of a lot more experienced in sleeping around than you happen to be. You gave me the gift of your innocence last night, a gift I don't deserve. On one hand I'd be some kind of idiot if I didn't admit a certain feeling of triumph that I could awaken such a response in you. On the other, I feel guilty as hell for having done so. And that, my blue-eyed witch, is what I was thinking about before daylight this morning as I stole like a thief from your bed."

"I must confess, that's about the last thing I expected to hear from you," Shena said quietly, staring at him. "Though I would like to point out that I invited you, remember? And if I don't feel any guilt, then why should you?"

"Therein lies the problem, sweetheart," Max muttered on a long sigh. "You've asked for nothing from me. You've given. I'm not accustomed to dealing with a woman like you." He smiled at her in such a way as to make Shena wonder how on earth she'd ever thought him to be stern and forbidding or even ugly. "And I do mean woman, in every sense of the word. So dismiss whatever thoughts you might be harboring that you were a disappointment in bed. Leaving you this morning was the most difficult thing I've ever done. If you knew me better, you'd know that remark isn't to be taken lightly."

"Thank you, Max."

"Will you have dinner with me this evening?"

"Why?"

"Because I would like to take you out," he said simply. "We've fought together and we've made love together, but we've yet to do something as simple as go out to dinner together."

"I'd be happy to have dinner with you." Shena smiled, then surprised Max by rising on tiptoe and kissing him. "In spite of your infuriating manners and your highly suspicious life-style, Max Cramer, you are a very nice person. Pick me up around seven."

Max caught her tightly in his arms, her openness washing over him like a breath of fresh air. Watch it! the voice of caution that had seen him through any number of difficult maneuvers prodded him. You aren't ready to settle down to a staid life of marriage and kids. If you aren't careful, Shena McLean will be leading you down the garden path by a two-inch ring in your nose.

The next few days in Shena's life were spent with each waking moment being devoted to thoughts of Max. He took her out to dinner each evening. They went for long drives afterward or went walking in some quiet spot. Though it was never discussed, there seemed to be an unspoken desire in them both to be alone together. On more than one occasion Max spent the night at Shena's cabin. He finished the work on the deck. Shena grew accustomed to his drop-in visits at the nursery, and often found him doing odds and ends repairs on the greenhouse or carrying the purchases of customers to their cars.

He was becoming a part of her life, a fact that left her with mixed emotions. They'd both entered into the relationship with the full understanding that it wasn't to go beyond the bounds of an affair. But as each day passed, Shena found herself comparing her life before she met Max to her life now, with Max in it. It was frightening to think that ending the affair wouldn't necessarily end her feelings for him.

"Aren't you seeing Max Cramer rather steadily these days?" Win asked Shena. It was Friday, and he had asked her out to lunch.

"I am." She took a sip of iced tea and thoughtfully looked at her friend over the rim of the glass. "You don't approve?"

"Oh no," Win quickly assured her. "I have no objections. Although I do think you should realize that he's not likely to be here much longer."

"Really?" Shena tried to appear unconcerned, but her heart was pounding like crazy. "What makes you think that?"

"Just listening to Max and putting two and two together." Win neatly evaded a direct answer. "I think he's probably finding the local scenery a bit dull."

"Oh well"—Shena shrugged—"I'll miss him when he goes. He's certainly turned my summer into something memorable. How's the world of banking?" she asked innocently. But at that moment she didn't care if every bank in the world failed. Win had merely expressed aloud the same thoughts she had been hiding in her heart. Unfortunately, hearing his suspicions only added to the sense of dread that had become her constant companion. What would she do if Max left?

CHAPTER TEN

Fred listened to the abrasive tone of his employer's voice as he shouted angrily into the phone. Max was mad as hell at somebody and Fred had a feeling heads were about to roll.

"Something wrong?" he asked calmly as the sound of the receiver being banged into place reverberated throughout the room.

"I'm beginning to wonder how this operation has gone on as long as it has." Max scowled as he rose to his feet and began pacing about the kitchen. "As I'm sure you know by now, that was Harrison on the phone. It seems he's authorized the sale to come off tonight."

"Tonight?" Fred's stern face appeared troubled. "That's pushing it forward by five or six days, isn't it?"

"At least." Max shook his head in disbelief. "It also means that after tonight, our work here will be finished."

For once Fred didn't come back with one of his caustic rejoinders. He couldn't decide what Max was

156

more upset about—having their work pushed ahead by a few days or that beginning the next day they would no longer have Shena McLean as a neighbor.

"I'll start packing this afternoon," Fred said hesitantly. "That should enable us to get an early start tomorrow."

"Don't bother packing for me." Max swung around and frowned at him. "If you want to get back to New York, feel free to leave at any time."

"What about you?" Fred asked. "Do you plan on taking a few days vacation before returning?"

"Not a vacation, Fred, and you can stop fishing," Max hurled at him. "After an overnight trip to D.C. and New York, I plan to spend as much time as I can with Shena."

"I see." Fred smiled as he continued basting the chicken he was preparing for dinner. "Am I to conclude from that statement that Miss McLean is going to become a part of our little family?"

"Now, how the hell would I know that? A woman's mind is as screwy and unpredictable as a box of broken springs."

"But if a man is really interested in finding a specific spring, he'll take the time to sort through all the different springs till he finds exactly what he's looking for, won't he?"

"Damned if I know, Fred."

"You don't?" the older man asked wryly.

"Hell, no." Max glared at him. "And to be quite

honest, I'm more frightened of the outcome with Shena than of the one tonight."

"Love can do that to some men."

"Love?" Max sneered.

"Of course," Fred said patiently. "For the first time since I've known you, you're worried about a woman." He shook his balding head. "That is definitely not you, Max. In the past, your idea of saying good-bye was a good dinner, a dozen roses and perhaps a small trinket to show your appreciation. This is the first time you've wanted to hang around, and for what? The lady in question thinks you're a criminal and that I am your accomplice." He gave a long, thoughtful pull at his chin with one hand. "I'm aware that your relationship with Shena has developed beyond that of a casual neighbor. But if I were you, I'd think it over carefully before I jumped."

"Oh?" Max scoffed.

"Shena is different. She's got matrimony written all over her."

"That's where you're wrong, Mr. Fix-it." The two of them glared at each other.

"Then what on earth is the problem? Either you want to marry her or you don't." Fred frowned. "I seriously doubt she's willing to live indefinitely with the sort of arrangement the two of you have now. Or are you planning on making extended visits to this part of the country in the future?"

"As much as it galls me to have to tell you this, Fred"—Max stared stonily out the window—"I don't

158

know what the hell I want. Things would have gone a lot smoother this summer if Shena McLean hadn't been living next door."

"Frankly, I like her," said Fred.

So do I, Max thought grimly—too damn much.

Shena glanced at the clock. It was seven forty-five. Max was thirty minutes late. She reached for the phone, then drew back. Surely if something had come up he'd have called. With a sense of unrest, she looked about the kitchen for something to do until he arrived.

Making cookies was out of the question, she thought. He would probably arrive just as she was ready to start baking. Her gaze fell on the potted plants. That was a safe enough chore to keep her busy.

It took her ten minutes to go through the cabin, carefully watering each of the plants. That out of the way, she walked out onto the deck and looked toward Max's cabin. There was still no sign of the Bronco. With a disgusted toss of her auburn head, she went back inside. She owed letters to two friends. Now would be the perfect time to get that obligation out of the way. And if Mr. Cramer hadn't contacted her by then, he could have dinner by himself!

When nine-thirty rolled around, Shena stamped angrily to her room and removed the attractive blue dress and the high-heeled sandals she'd been wearing. As far as she was concerned, she had been stood up, and Max could take a flying leap into Willow Creek.

It was way past midnight before she fell exhausted into bed. In the interim, Shena had cleaned out the fridge, baked a batch of cookies, vacuumed the entire cabin and cleaned the bathroom till the tiles almost groaned in protest. As she stretched her tired body against the cool sheets, she found her back aching from the frantic pace she'd set for herself and her head pounding as if a drum were within her skull.

Sleep, when it did come, was filled with dreams of Max. Alternately she was in Max's arms or scornfully ignoring him as he pleaded with her to forgive him. In her dream his movements were hampered by the large ball and chain attached to his ankle, his huge frame clothed in prison garb.

The next morning found a bleary-eyed Shena up long before the alarm sounded. Before leaving for work, she made many trips to the kitchen window in hopes of seeing the Bronco parked in front of Max's cabin. But the driveway was empty.

Her arrival at work, and the determined set of her small chin, drew looks of speculation from Chloe and Charlie. As the morning progressed and Shena's mood steadily deteriorated, they drew a simultaneous breath of relief when she disappeared into the office and slammed the door.

Shena dropped into a rickety old chair and leaned back with a weary sigh. She hadn't expected any wild declarations of love from Max, she told herself, hadn't expected any promises spoken at a time when emotions were peaked. But neither had she expected to be ignored.

But that's what you get when you cast your lot with a man you've distrusted from the start, her conscience jabbed at her. You've only yourself to blame for the hurt that's gnawing at you.

She reached for a tissue in her pocket and blotted the tears that were running down her cheeks. No, she thought dejectedly, she hadn't expected anything, but she had unconsciously hoped for so much —too much.

The love for Max she'd been refusing to acknowledge rushed forward and swelled within her heart like a river overflowing its banks. She was furious at him for having stood her up but, at the same time, she was frantic with worry for him.

When the telephone rang, she reached for it quickly. "Hello?"

"Shena? Are you busy?" Win asked.

"So, so," she remarked flatly. "What's on your mind?"

"Er—I need to see you."

"Now?"

"Now. Can you come to my office or would you rather go somewhere and grab a cup of coffee?"

A sinking feeling rushed over Shena. Win was never serious unless it concerned bank business. She wondered what financial crisis was about to befall her. "Let's have coffee. Your office always makes me nervous." She tried for a joking tone. When Win didn't respond in kind, she knew she was in trouble.

Fifteen minutes later she met Win in a small restaurant in one of the malls where they often had lunch. There was a fixed smile on Shena's face as she slipped into the booth.

"Hmm, you do look serious," she observed resignedly as she got a good look at his round face.

"I'm afraid I am, honey." He waited until the waitress set the coffee he'd ordered before them. When they were alone, he opened his briefcase and removed the morning newspaper. "I know you seldom read your paper, so I brought you this one." He slid it across the table, his pudgy forefinger pointing to an article. On the same page was a fuzzy photo showing several men. Some were casually dressed and three others were in law-enforcement uniforms. Win looked at Shena with soulful eyes. "Believe me, honey, I hate this almost as much as you do. I'd gotten to know the damn fool and I really liked him."

The heading of the article read, "Southeastern Heavy Equipment Ring Broken Up by Authorities." Shena felt the cold hand of fear gripping her heart as she scanned the more pertinent details, then let her gaze slip over the faces of the men pictured and their names. Nothing could disguise his size. And though his face wasn't clear, Shena knew in her very soul that it was Max's face peering back over his shoulder

162

as he'd obviously been trying to escape the camera's eye.

She raised eyes brimming with tears to meet Win's sympathetic ones. "I—I suppose William Cox is an alias, isn't it? Or do you suppose Max Cramer is the alias?"

Win sighed, his lips drawn tightly together. "I don't know, honey." He reached across the table and caught her hands in his. "Do you want me to see what I can find out for you?"

Shena's first reaction was to say no. No, no, no, a thousand times. But something wouldn't let her. "Please," she said quietly. "And, Win, will you check and see if I can visit him?"

"I don't think that's wise, Shena."

"Perhaps not, but I have to do it."

"All right, I'll do it only if you promise me one thing." He looked stern.

"What's that?"

"Go home. Chloe and Charlie can take care of the shop. You go home and I'll be out later with whatever news I have for you and a quart of Mother's soup." He gave her a smile that brought a new rush of tears to her eyes. "Don't worry, squirt, we'll see this thing through together."

For once Shena didn't argue with his suggestion. She couldn't. She had to go home to find some kind of relief.

But the cabin, instead of giving her comfort, thrust the memory of Max boldly into focus. In the bedroom she closed her eyes and saw him in the bed. A shirt of his was neatly folded and lying on the chair. He'd forgotten it after one of their nights together. Shena looked at it now and couldn't keep from shivering.

Throughout the entire cabin there were reminders of him. He'd fixed the door on the pantry, hung the wooden towel racks in the bathroom. They'd spent one entire Saturday applying the weather-resistant coating to the deck he'd finished. Even at that moment she was staring at a single white rose he'd brought her two days ago.

But you knew, her conscience kept hammering away at her, you knew.

Yes, she silently acknowledged as she stared unseeingly out the window at the cool, cloudy day. She had known not to trust him, but love had slipped in anyway. Her defenses against his charms had been equal to fragile silk being caught in the grip of a raging storm—merely a pretense of resistance against such a formidable strength. For a storm was how she saw Max, strong, swift, powerful—and destructive.

Unmindful of the tears that seemed to have no end to their flow, Shena walked into the bedroom and fell across the bed. She doubted that she could sleep, but within minutes her body was relaxed and her breathing was even.

The pounding on the front door of the cabin brought a startled Shena to her feet like a shot. Win! Still a bit dazed from her nap, she collected her thoughts together enough to wobble her way to the front door and open it.

"Well, I must say, it took you long enough to get here," her friend scolded. He looked like a delivery boy, with both arms loaded with an assortment of brown bags. Ashamed at her lack of manners, Shena reached out and relieved Win of some of his packages.

"I'm sorry I took so long, I was sleeping," she remarked as she turned and headed for the kitchen.

"That's good," Win replied as he followed her.

The next few minutes were spent unearthing his plans for their dinner. "Mother's soup," he quipped as he set out a quart of the homemade soup. "You can have a small bowl now, but I picked up steaks for our dinner." He placed the steaks and two large Idaho potatoes on the counter, along with a quart of ice cream, an apple pie and a bag of yeast rolls from a local bakery. "You do have the makings for a salad, don't you?"

Shena stared at the man before her, blinking back tears. "Has anyone ever told you what a nice person you are, Win?"

He gave her a direct look from beneath comically drawn-together blond brows. "Are you sure you're okay, squirt?" He frowned. "I've known you practically all your life, and when you start raining words of praise upon my head it usually means trouble."

"There's no ulterior motive, I promise," Shena said quietly. "In fact, I don't know why I'm saying these things for I know what a pain you can be, but you're also my dearest friend. I just feel like thanking you for what you've done and are doing for me."

Win leaned forward and gave her a loud smack on the cheek. He hoped that might pull her out of her mood and make her yell at him. "Consider me thanked, then move your skinny behind out of my way. I have things to do, woman. By the way," he said casually as he rummaged around for a saucepan in which to heat the soup, "do you think you can take another shock?"

Shena spun around to stare at him, her heart jumping to her throat. She'd deliberately put off asking about Max. "You know where he is?" she asked in a quavering voice.

Win seemed undecided for a moment. Finally, he reached into one of the bags still on the counter and took out a magazine. Shena recognized it as a national publication dealing with the world of finance and the wizards behind the multimillion-dollar schemes. Win quickly flipped through the pages until he found the one he was searching for. "Perhaps you'd better sit down, Shena," he advised as he handed her the magazine.

At first Shena ignored his words of warning. But she sank heavily onto the chair when she found herself staring into the harsh, stern face of Max Cramer from the page of the magazine, and a heading that read, "Financial Genius Wins Board Battle." She looked up at Win, her expression one of complete bafflement. "I don't understand," she said faintly.

"I didn't either, at first. Read the article while your soup's heating, then I'll explain it to you."

Like an obedient child, Shena did as instructed. She read of the successes Max had enjoyed since his first acquisition of a small, floundering company a number of years ago. One after another his accomplishments were listed, along with an estimate, by the author of the column, of Max's personal worth. Shena read and reread the amount at least half a dozen times. She had never considered him to be a pauper, but neither had she ever imagined him to be rich as Midas—at least not legitimately.

Win plunked the soup before her, along with a spoon and some crackers. He took the magazine from her unresisting hands. "No sense reading it until the print disappears, toots, it's all there in black and white."

"But what does it mean?" she cried out in confusion.

"It means your Max Cramer and that Max Cramer"—he pointed to the article as he sat down—"are one and the same."

"Have you forgotten William Cox?"

"Not at all. Look at this." Win placed yet another newspaper before her. "Wealthy Executive Goes Undercover for Gov't in Theft Ring," the headline read.

The more she read, the more her grief began to turn to pure unadulterated rage. She'd spent last night and the better part of the day imagining all sorts of terrible things happening to Max Cramer, and all the while that jerk had been out chasing some idiot who'd stolen a road grader! And his squinty-eyed friend, Fred, was no better. He'd been a picture of innocence during their entire stay in Florida, while protecting his boss from any danger.

"I'll kill that revolting bastard!" she exclaimed, a murderous glint in her blue eyes.

"Don't you think it would be best if you waited to hear his side of the story first?" Win suggested hopefully. He'd seen kinder, more compassionate expressions on the faces of angry tigers at the local zoo.

"As far as I'm concerned he doesn't have a side," Shena declared. "He had ample opportunity to fill me in on his little scheme and his life. It wasn't necessary for me to learn about it through every national publication in the nation."

"Well"—Win shrugged, a grin of amusement spreading over his face—"at least you can't classify him as a worthless drifter."

"How comforting," Shena said bitingly. "Next you'll be telling me that I should catch the first plane to wherever it is he's hiding and beg his forgiveness for ever doubting him."

"I must admit that would be right neighborly of you," Win said with a straight face. "Would you like me to make plane reservations for you?"

"No, you uncaring fink." Shena glowered at him.

"If you keep this up, you can take your steak and potatoes and leave."

"What about my soup?"

"Leave the soup, I love your mother's cooking."

The ringing of the telephone interrupted their lively exchange. At a motion from Shena, Win answered.

"Max?" he said, looking inquisitively at Shena. "Er —yes, she's here. Yes"—he nodded—"we saw the paper . . . several of them in fact, and the magazine article. Hang on a minute, Max, and let me get her." He pressed his hand over the mouthpiece and hissed at Shena, "He wants to talk to you."

"Tell him to go to hell!"

"Shena!"

"You heard me, Win," she said stubbornly. "Nothing on earth could induce me to talk to that fink. I never want to see him again, and I hope some hobo burns his cabin to the ground."

"Ahem . . . er, Max." Win was literally squirming with embarrassment. "I can't seem to find Shena. She must have stepped out. Do you want me to have her call you? Oh—well, good luck to you."

"What did he say?" Shena demanded the moment the connection was broken.

"A number of things. Most of which had to do with your being related to a mule."

"The coward."

"Not necessarily. He said to tell you that he would see you tomorrow."

169

The next morning found a grim-faced Shena going about her work with a watchful air governing her every move. By ten thirty she was jumpy as a cat, acting as though she expected Max to spring out at her from behind every tree and shrub she walked past. When the sprinkler system went on the blink, she surprised Charlie by telling him she would do the watering. It was a boring chore, but it would keep her busy and out of reach of the customers.

Shena was giving a new shipment of ornamental shrubs a good soaking when she sensed that she wasn't alone. She turned her head and glanced over her shoulder. The shock of seeing Max only a few feet behind her left her pale and shaken.

"Hello, Shena," he said in his deep, raspy voice. He was dressed differently from what she was accustomed to. Gone were the scruffy jeans and the tattered canvas shoes. Now he was dressed like the successful executive he was. He looked tough and uncompromising, and the general air of authority emanating from him stirred an angry response in Shena.

"Get off my property, Mr. Cramer," she said stiffly. He was standing firm and determined not far from her.

"Not until we talk," he said just as determinedly, then began to move toward her.

Without thinking of the outcome, Shena whirled around and aimed the hose directly toward him. Her

170

thumb released the lever on the hand sprinkler that controlled the flow, sending a rushing gush of water that hit Max directly in the chest. She saw him throw up his hands in an effort to keep the blast from hitting him in the face. The air was turned blue with the explosive burst of curse words that erupted from his lips, and Shena wondered if she'd been perhaps hasty in her desire for retribution. During the melee and while she was deciding which would be the quickest exit from her place of business, she was aware of Chloe and Charlie as they stood watching her, their mouths hanging open in astonishment.

Without further thought to her plan of escape, Shena heaved the heavy hose as hard as she could toward Max, then turned on her heel and raced for the back gate behind the office. Her car was parked just outside the eight-foot chain-link fence that surrounded her business. Just as she reached the corner, she allowed herself one quick peek over her shoulder. What she saw would have been comical if only she'd had the time to enjoy it.

Max was lying spread-eagled on the asphalt walkway. There was at least five pounds of sawdust and potting soil smeared from the top of his head to the soles of his expensive shoes. He was cursing in a loud, thunderous voice and yelling for a bug-eyed Charlie to "Do something with this damned hose before I cram it down your throat!"

There would always be a special love in her heart for the ugly little VW, Shena vowed as she literally vaulted into the driver's seat and turned the key. The engine started on the first try. And though her departure from the scene of the crime wasn't dignified in the least, it was definitely the swiftest.

But where to go? Shena thought wildly as she darted in and out of traffic like a maniac. Win's apartment? She had a key. There were several other friends' places where she knew she would be welcome. But would it be fair to involve them in her fight with Max? she asked herself. No, she quickly decided, and made the turn onto the access road to the interstate on two protesting wheels. She'd fight him on her own turf.

Mercifully, the cabin was reached before any personal injury from an automobile accident befell her. The gasping, heaving little car belched to a stop in front of the cabin and Shena was out and flying toward the front door without even pulling the emergency brake. Had she had the forethought to look behind her, she would have seen her little car gathering momentum as it headed for the banks of Willow Creek. By the time the VW hit the water, the front door to the house was slammed and locked and Shena was racing frantically from room to room securing the windows and the other remaining door.

Once the house was locked up tight, she dropped into a chair at the kitchen table and raised shaking hands to her face. Her heart was racing like a runaway engine and her breathing was reduced to short gulps. Oh Lord! Any minute she was expecting to hear the sound of Max tearing down the door, log by log.

A drink. She needed a drink, she told herself. With shaky hands, she drew out Chloe's "wine" and poured a generous portion into an ice-tea glass. She left room enough for a couple of ice cubes, but in her haste to settle her nerves, she forgot to add them and took a healthy sip.

She was on fire. Her eyes crossed, fluttered and uncrossed in rapid succession. Each individual hair on her head stood on end and waved to its neighbor. The enamel on her teeth seemed to be washed away with one fell swoop! Not wanting to go through life in such a decidedly freaky condition, she raised the glass to her lips once again in an attempt to set the world upright and to restore her body to its rightful state of being.

The second drink of "wine" did wonders for Shena's state of mind. The third one had her positively floating when she walked, which she was doing quite a bit of as she peered out the windows, looking for Max's car. The fourth drink was taken to reenforce the feeling of power she was beginning to feel as she strode about her tiny, secured kingdom uttering scathing words of abuse upon the head of the man she'd once loved.

CHAPTER ELEVEN

Shena frowned. It seemed to her, in her befuddled state, that Max had had ample time to make the drive from town. She glanced hazily about her, her small chin tilted in defiance. "Well," she said haughtily, "if he gives up that easily, then to hell with him!"

On an impulse, she picked up her glass and made her way to the back door. After a brief battle with the lock, she emerged victorious from the cabin and walked out onto the deck.

The first thing she saw as she left her fortress was the neighboring cabin. Her space was becoming too crowded, she decided imperiously. She would have that hovel leveled. It would serve two purposes. It would ensure her of complete privacy and, at the same time, remove any reminders of the man who had ruined her summer.

Perhaps she should sit, she thought as she breathed deep breaths of fresh air. She turned, too swiftly, and frowned. She must be seeing things. What else could account for her thinking she saw Max Cramer's menacing form sprawled in her one and only lounge chair? She blinked her eyes and continued across the deck toward the other chair. The closer she got to her goal, the clearer the illusion became.

Suddenly Shena came to a precarious halt. She grasped the back of the chair with one hand, the hand holding the glass dropping to her side. She ignored the trickle of clear liquid that trickled down the side of her jeans and into her shoe as she stared intently at Max.

"You're trespassing," she stated icily.

"Sue me," Max replied with a trace of a smile softening his features.

"You have no right to enter my . . . my space," she informed him grandly. The hand holding the glass jerked up to add conviction to her words and the glass sailed through the air toward Max like a guided missile.

He caught the glass and set it on the floor, then swung his feet to the floor and stood. By the time Shena decided she should make a hasty retreat back inside to safety, she felt the weight of Max's hands on her shoulders.

"I forbid you to touch me." She frowned. He was so close, her neck was tilted back to her shoulders. She was determined to look him dead in the eye.

"But if I don't touch you, Shena, you'll fall and hurt yourself," he pointed out with a gleam of amusement in his tawny eyes. He leaned down and sniffed. "Been sampling the wine again?"

"Certainly not," she replied stiffly. "I merely had a

drink to settle my nerves. It's not every day that a woman finds out the man she loves is a thief and reads of his capture in the morning paper."

Max turned her around and began guiding her back inside the cabin. "But shouldn't the woman be happy when she learns that the man she loves is not a thief but a hardworking individual who obeys the law?" He continued their progress through the kitchen and down the tiny hall.

"Not when he's stood her up the evening before." Shena scowled. Her head was beginning to swim and it was getting harder and harder to concentrate. "Besides that, the fink is stinking rich."

"Wouldn't you enjoy spending some of the fink's money?" He grinned as he steered her into the bathroom.

"I don't think I'll ever be able to forgive him for being so closemouthed about it. You kept everything about your life a secret!" she accused.

"It wouldn't have been safe to tell you about what I was doing," Max replied.

Shena blinked her eyes and looked groggily about her. "Why on earth are we in the bathroom?"

"It's simple, my darling Miss McLean. We're going to take a shower." He removed one hand long enough to reach inside and adjust the water. He turned back to Shena and began removing her clothes.

"Take your hands off me," she spluttered in face of

the cold draft that hit her when her blouse was jerked off her arms. "I'll get pneumonia," she wailed.

"That's not bloody likely," Max said dryly. He held her squirming body with one hand while he unfastened her slacks with the other hand and pushed them down over her hips and legs. "You've consumed enough antifreeze to protect you in the Arctic." Her bra and panties were added to the heap of clothing on the floor. Max held her wriggling body away from him for a moment, slowly shaking his shaggy head as he stared into her vague but stormy eyes. "You are without a doubt the most bullheaded little bit of baggage I've ever met." He slipped out of his own jeans and briefs, then lifted Shena and stepped into the shower.

"Aaahh," she screamed as the ice-cold water peppered down on her naked body. "I'm freezing to death."

"Nothing so dramatic, I assure you." Max grinned. He held her directly beneath the spray with one hand, the other hand running over her body with a bar of perfumed soap. "Since you were considerate enough to give me a shower earlier, I think it only neighborly to return the favor."

"You are a pig! An uncaring, insensitive, double-dealing brute!" she yelled at him. "Let me out of this damn shower. I'm dying from the cold!"

"Pipe down and stop cursing." Max frowned at her.

"I will not pipe down, you twerp." She glared at

177

him through several strands of sopping-wet hair. "And if you're thinking of taking me to bed, you can damn well forget it. Right now, sex is the farthest thing from my mind."

"Frankly, my dear Shena, at the moment I'm about as interested in your body as I am a case of the measles. You look awful and you smell worse. So put your mind at ease. I'm only concerned with one thing— sobering you up."

Even in her drunken state, which was quickly disappearing thanks to the ice-cold water, she knew when she had been bested.

Standing before a mirror sometime later, Shena decided the reflection that stared back was that of a reasonably attractive woman. Her hair was shiny and in its usual curly state after the shampoo Max had given her. The nap he'd insisted she take had whisked away the signs of fatigue that had been so visible earlier. Makeup had been used sparingly. She'd even opted for a blue caftan rather than slacks. All in all, she looked nice.

The sounds and scents coming from the kitchen made Shena hang back. She would have to face Max, but she wanted to put it off as long as possible. Ever since she'd rammed his car with her pickup, and even today when she'd sprayed him with the hose, each of her escapades had ended with trouble for her. And as for feelings, she mused, she'd come out behind there, too.

Max had deceived her. Perhaps not willingly, but

he'd done so nonetheless. He had been mysterious about his life and his job. He'd let her believe the very worst about him and never once tried to set her mind at ease. She turned to leave the bedroom. He had a lot of explaining to do.

"You look rested," Max told her as he held her chair out for her, then walked back over to the counter.

"I feel much better, thank you."

"Good. Because I don't want to see a crumb of food left on your plate," he said as he set a steak and sizzling french fries before her. There was a salad and rolls already on the table.

"This is enough for two people," she protested.

Max sat down next to her, a heavy scowl pulling at his lips. "I'm getting extremely tired of arguing with you, Miss McLean. Eat."

"Go sit on a tack." She grinned at him as she popped a fry into her mouth. "Oooh." Her eyes grew round as saucers. She grabbed her glass of water and gulped it down. "That was hot," she said when she could talk, grimacing.

"Sorry, I should have warned you."

"You should have warned me three months ago, when I first asked you what you were doing in Florida," Shena said sweetly. Their gazes locked and it was Max who looked away first.

"The people I was involved with weren't very nice people, Shena," he explained. "Your life could have been in danger if I'd told you what I was doing. Don't you remember me telling you this earlier?"

"How could I? You held me under that freezing jet of water till my skin turned blue."

Max laid down his fork and looked at her, hiding a smile. "And a more ungrateful brat I've yet to encounter. You were also noisy and your language was terrible."

"Dear me," Shena answered in feigned distress. "Isn't there anything about me that pleases you?"

"You know what pleases me, Shena love," he murmured, then chuckled at the rush of red that crept over her face. "Shall I enumerate each and every little detail?"

"Pig!" she muttered disdainfully. She picked up her knife and fork and began working on the steak. "I hope Win won't mind you eating his steak."

"So do I. Why didn't he eat it himself?"

"Oh he intended to, last night, but he made the mistake of showing me several articles regarding your patriotism and your enormous wealth. After that, I lost my appetite and he decided to go home."

Max chuckled. "I can't decide if you're more angry with me for not telling you the reason I'm in Florida or for not telling you of my wealth. Do you even know?"

"They run neck and neck."

"Don't you like the idea of never having to worry about money again?" he asked curiously.

"Well, who wouldn't? But the way you tried to hide it from me makes me feel as if you suspected me of being some kind of money-hungry bitch."

180

Max reached out and caught her chin in a firm grasp. "Don't you ever let me hear you say that again," he ordered. "I never once thought you wanted anything from me."

"How could you have?" Shena frowned at him. "I had no idea you were hoarding a fortune. Now that I know . . ." She let her voice trail off.

"Yes?" he asked smoothly.

"Why don't I make you a list of the things I want? It would be much easier."

"Do that. By the way, I've done my last stint as an undercover agent," he threw in casually. Shena didn't say anything, but she felt a sense of profound relief slip over her. "Does that please you?"

"Yes," she murmured. "But it had to be your decision. I would never have asked you to give it up."

"Why not?"

"We made an agreement, remember?" She forced her eyes to meet his. "We said at the outset there would be no restrictions, no entanglements. I prefer to keep it that way."

"Well, I sure as hell don't," Max snapped. His look of anger startled Shena. "I wouldn't hesitate asking you to give up something for me."

"But what do I have that I could give up? I'm not a spy, nor am I wealthy, Max," she quietly explained as though talking to a child. "My only lover has been you, so even there you can hardly go about demanding that I give up the other men in my life."

"No," he said quietly, "I know full well there's no

other man in your life." He let his gaze slide over the room, then back to her. "But you love this cabin. Would you give it up for me? You love your business. Would you leave it and come with me?"

"Probably—if you asked me," Shena said simply.

"Still with no strings attached?" he asked carefully, and felt the hairs on his neck stand out as he waited for her answer.

"No strings, Max."

"And if I had one or two I'd like to attach to the relationship? What would be your answer?" He still couldn't believe it. Max couldn't believe Shena was for real. She wanted nothing from him but his love.

"I love you, but I still have my dignity," she replied without batting an eye. "It's fifty-fifty or nothing at all."

"You drive a hard bargain," he sighed as though weary from the struggle. "But"—he reached into his shirt pocket and removed a tiny object that twinkled —"I suppose I'll be forced to give in."

Shena watched, hypnotized, as he caught her left hand in his and slipped a gorgeous diamond solitaire onto her finger. She stared at the ring, then raised a questioning face to him. "Where I come from, when a man gives a woman a ring such as this one, it usually means something quite different from an affair."

"Is that right?" Max drawled. He leaned forward and caught her face between his hands and kissed her, his lips hard, but gentle. "Then I suppose you'll just have to take advantage of me, won't you? I mean

—since I've never done this sort of thing and all
. . ."

Shena smiled like a kitten who's just enjoyed a
large saucer of cream. She leaned back in her chair,
holding her hand out before her in unashamed admiration of the ring. She cast a devilish grin at her
intended. "Say it, Max."

He frowned. "If I do, my teeth will fall out."

"With your money you can afford dentures. I intend to have all that goes with it. Talk, you spineless
wimp."

"I love you." He glared at her.

"You're repeating yourself. You told me that earlier, when you put me to bed. Pop the question,
buster, I'm greedy."

"You're a shameless wench."

"I know." She smiled kindly at him. "But I'd like to
be your wench—if you have the courage to utter four
little words. Man or mouse, Max. I don't have all
day." She eyed him briskly. "These days, a girl has to
protect herself from all sides."

"Will . . . will you marry me?" came the faltering
question.

For one insane moment, Shena fought to control
her laughter at the stricken expression on his face.
"I'm not sure." She returned his disbelieving stare.
"As you once pointed out, I'm much younger than
you. You're more experienced. How am I to know
whether or not I'm getting a bargain in you?"

"You make me sound like a damn car!" he bellowed.

"Well, from the excellent way in which you make love, I think it's fair to say you've probably got more mileage on you than a Greyhound bus. So why don't you use some of that expertise in convincing me?"

Max had been goaded beyond his limits. He rose to his feet, his chair crashing against the floor. In one fell swoop, he bent and caught Shena in his arms and carried her to the bedroom. Instead of dropping her on the bed, he stood her on the floor and removed the caftan before she could blink an eye. He hooked his thumb beneath the waistband of the sheer bikini briefs and eased them to her feet, his lips touching each inch of skin en route.

Shena reached out and grasped him for support as his lips made the same trail along her body on the return journey. She felt her nipples tightening against the roughness of his shirt as it brushed against her breasts. His hands left her then. She watched eagerly while Max shrugged out of his clothes.

They stared at each other, their eyes touching intimately on their naked bodies. Shena reached a tentative hand toward his hip, the tips of her fingers caressing the warm tanned skin. When she would have pulled away, Max stopped her. He caught her hand and carried it to that part of him that brought so much pleasure to her.

"Don't be shy, Shena love. Touch me," he whispered hoarsely. "It works both ways, you know."

With his gentle urgings in her ear, she gave in to his bidding, barely able to control herself as she saw Max's head drop back on his shoulders and heard the swift intake of air into his lungs. An intoxicating headiness floated over her at her power to arouse him. It touched her that contrary to his seemingly unyielding character, he was so gentle and understanding with her.

As if seeing into her mind, Max drew her to him and they fell in a tangled heap to the bed. His hands cupped and palmed the tingling softness of her breasts while his tongue sucked and teased each excited nipple. There was nothing rushed or hurried as each point of arousal was favored with the lingering caress of his tongue.

Shena's hands grasped the sheet and her eyes were tightly closed against the continuous surge of desire that washed over her. From her hair to the tips of her toes, up and down, over and over, the erotic homage to her body was paid.

Finally she felt Max move up over her. She opened her eyes to meet his passion-filled ones. "Are you sorry now for all those unkind things you said to me?" he rasped, his tongue licking its way to the corner of her mouth.

"Later," she gasped. "I'll think about it later. Make love to me, Max."

And he did, his body slipping into place and the thrust of his thighs against her filling her with a joy that threw her, then left her suspended in space.

Where only moments ago he had been patient and gentle, there was now a sense of urgency about Max that matched the fierce need in Shena. Their hunger for each other was raw and primitive, their bodies in search of a gratification that brought the world exploding into a billion shimmering pieces and then left them limp with exhaustion.

Sometime later, when Shena opened sleepy eyes, she met the amused gleam of Max's steady brown ones. He was propped on one elbow staring down at her.

"I love you, Shena McLean," he murmured in a rough voice that didn't quite hide the wealth of tenderness beneath.

"I know." Shena smiled gently. "You told me several times when you were tucking me in bed for my nap. You also stood me up night before last."

"I explained that to you as well," he sighed heavily. "I tried to call you, but your line at work was busy. After the fourth try, I dropped Fred off at the airport, then hurried to meet the authorities."

"You couldn't have trusted me with even a little bit of what you were doing?"

"No. I couldn't take a chance on your becoming involved. You're too precious to me." He grinned. "Even then, when I was fighting the idea of marriage like the plague, you meant more than life to me." He dropped back against the bed, pulling Shena with him. "Marry me as soon as we can arrange it."

"I will."

"Good. Can you be ready to leave in an hour?"

"An hour?" Shena squeaked.

"Of course," Max said innocently. "You don't expect me to wait indefinitely, do you?"

"You poor, deprived thing," she murmured with a sparkle in her eyes. Suddenly a sobering expression crowded her features. "What about my cabin and my business?"

"Why don't we have my cabin moved, and added to yours?" Max suggested. "As for your business, perhaps you could work something out with Chloe. I'd never insist that you give it up, but I hope you'll want to spend as much time with me in New York as I want to with you."

"Very shrewd, Mr. Cramer." Shena grinned. "Very shrewd. May I call Win and tell him our plans?"

"We'll take him with us if it will make you happy. Close the shop and take Chloe and Charlie as well. I don't care if the whole damn world is there for our wedding. Although to be truthful"—he tried to be stern—"I think I've been married to you in my mind since that day you ran over me in that awful pickup."

"You shouldn't say such unkind things about my vehicles."

"Speaking of your vehicle"—Max grinned—"are you aware that your VW is now resting in Willow Creek?"

"What?" Shena cried.

"Apparently you failed to pull the emergency brake when you arrived at the cabin. When I first saw the ugly color of the top sticking out of the creek, I almost died. My first thought was that you'd had an accident."

"Can it be gotten out?"

"I'm sure it can. But I don't think you'll be driving it again."

"Thank heavens," Shena sighed. "And thank you for the new car I think you're going to buy me." She leaned down and teased his lips with the moist tip of her tongue.

"Softening me up, Shena love?"

"Of course," she said pertly. "I want a baby-blue Mercedes."

"Then you've got about thirty minutes before we have to dress and leave in which to convince me to buy you one. Think you can do it?"

"It will be a piece of cake, Max darling, a piece of cake."

And it was!

Fans of

Heather Graham

*will delight
in her boldest
romance to date!*

Golden Surrender

Against her will, Ireland's Princess Erin is married off by her father to her sworn enemy, Prince Olaf of Norway. A Viking warrior, Olaf and his forces are needed by the High King to defeat the invading Danes.

Nevertheless, the proud princess vows that her heart and soul will never belong to her husband, although her body might. Until one day that body, together with the life of her young baby, is almost destroyed by the evil Danes. When her husband *proves* his deep and abiding love for Erin by braving a desperate rescue attempt, she is forced to admit that her heart also holds a fierce love for her brave husband. $3.50   12973-7-33

Don't forget Candlelight Ecstasies and Supremes for Heather Graham's other romances!

 At your local bookstore or use this handy coupon for ordering:

**DELL READERS SERVICE—DEPT. B744A
P.O. BOX 1000, PINE BROOK, N.J. 07058**

Please send me the above title(s). I am enclosing $_____ (please add 75c per copy to cover postage and handling). Send check or money order—no cash or CODs. Please allow 3-4 weeks for shipment. CANADIAN ORDERS: please submit in U.S. dollars.

Ms./Mrs./Mr._____

Address_____

City/State_____ Zip_____

JAYNE CASTLE

excites and delights you with
tales of adventure and romance

____TRADING SECRETS

Sabrina had wanted only a casual vacation fling with the
rugged Matt. But, the extraordinary pull between them
made that impossible. So did her growing relationship
with his son—and her daring attempt to save the boy's life.
19053-3-15 $3.50

____DOUBLE DEALING

Jayne Castle sweeps you into the corporate world of
multimillion dollar real estate schemes and the very
private world of executive lovers. Mixing business with
pleasure, they made *passion* their bottom line.
12121-3-18 $3.95

At your local bookstore or use this handy coupon for ordering:

DELL READERS SERVICE—DEPT. B744B
P.O. BOX 1000, PINE BROOK, N.J. 07058

Please send me the above title(s). I am enclosing $_____ (please add 75¢ per copy to cover
postage and handling). Send check or money order—no cash or COD's. Please allow 3-4 weeks for shipment.
CANADIAN ORDERS: please submit in U.S. dollars.

Ms. Mrs. Mr._____

Address_____

City State_____ Zip _____